Jit'Suku Chronicles
In the Stars

Heart of
the Machine

BIANCA D'ARC

This book is a work of fiction. The names, characters, places, and incidents are products of the writer's imagination or have been used fictitiously and are not to be construed as real. Any resemblance to persons, living or dead, actual events, locale or organizations is entirely coincidental.

No part of this book may be used or reproduced in any manner whatsoever without written permission, except in the case of brief quotations embodied in critical articles and reviews.

Copyright © 2019 Bianca D'Arc
Published by Hawk Publishing, LLC

Copyright © 2019 Bianca D'Arc

All rights reserved.

ISBN-13: 978-1-950196-23-4

Billie Latimer is the half-trained navigator on a ship full of refugees, crewed by cyborgs who are just starting to remember who they once were. It's heartbreaking, but she's glad to help the men who had everything stolen from them by the military machine. Especially one very special man, who has captured her interest - the captain of the ship. Working with him day after day only brings them closer. She suspects he's interested in her, as well, but something is keeping him from taking that final step closer.

Captain Medeus knew almost from the start that Billie is the sister of a man he had once called friend. A man who had died aboard Medeus's last ship. He blames himself and carries a lot of guilt, now that he remembers who he was. He's not sure it's fair to continue his pursuit of Billie, knowing she would blame him for the death of her beloved brother, if she knew.

With hostile aliens and the military ready to blow them to smithereens, not to mention pirates, there's a lot to contend with. Can they keep everyone safe and learn to live again in the chaotic world in which they find themselves? Neither is sure if they can forgive the past and start anew, or if misplaced guilt will keep them apart…forever.

DEDICATION

To Peggy McChesney, without whom there would have been a major error in this book. Peggy, you're the BEST!

Also, in honor of my Dad, a scientist who worked on the space program during the golden age of putting a man on the moon, and encouraged my love of science fiction from an early age.

PROLOGUE

Billie wondered again, why she'd ever thought a career as a navigator was a good idea. She'd only been halfway through her schooling when she'd been abandoned by the academy to which she'd given all her savings, in exchange for an accelerated course in interstellar navigation. They'd taken her money and left her high and dry on *Eagle Nest Station* when the alien jit'suku showed up and threatened to kill anyone who remained on the station after their deadline.

Billie and her little brother had taken their chances with a ship full of cyborgs who had also been abandoned by their military handlers. The elite on the station had taken every last ship, except one old relic that lay partially disassembled in a repair bay, and buggered off for Earth without looking back. They'd left hundreds of helpless people at the mercy of aliens who were well known for having none.

But the cyborgs had somehow gotten the ship working enough to shove off the station. Before they had left, though, they'd put out a call to invite anyone who wanted to go with them, to come aboard. Not seeing any other choice, Billie had gone with the cyborg who had been sent around the station to look for people who wanted to go with them. He'd helped her with her little brother, who was only nine, and couldn't run all the way across the station to the repair bay where the ship was docked. Not when she also had to bring their duffel bags, containing everything they owned.

When she'd finally arrived at the ship, the cyborg had escorted her straight to the captain, who had been busily overseeing the dockside. She'd showed the captain her reports from the academy and he'd asked her a few questions about her abilities before he decided to put her on the nav station. She'd had to share nav duties with a cyborg who, she had no doubt, checked all her math.

The cyborgs were thought to be mindless machines. Men—mostly soldiers—who had been so badly damaged in the ongoing war with the jit'suku that they had been rebuilt. They were given various cybernetic implants and the means to control them. Most people believed nothing of the human mind remained after the cybertronic control systems were implanted in the brain during the cyborginazation process. It was well documented that the biological part of the brain was subsumed by the Cybertronic Control System or CCS.

But, Billie was learning, something had changed. The cyborgs were evolving. They were *remembering*. They knew who they had once been. And, while they were still part machine and had computers in their brains, they were also remembering the human lives they had led. They'd been men of honor who had served humanity in the ongoing war.

Of course, now, they were weapons themselves. Their skeletal systems had been enhanced to carry the added weight of their implants. Their bodies had been rewired—no two of them alike. Each was unique, depending on what parts they had needed to have replaced and what the military medical machine had deemed necessary at the time.

The men had been stripped of their identities and basic human rights. They had been officially reclassified as Artificial Intelligences. They'd been given orders they could not countermand or question and had been sent back to the front lines to fight humanity's battle against the alien invaders.

It was sad, really. Now that Billie knew the men were remembering what had happened to them, she had a lot of compassion for their situation. Still, she found them intimidating, though her little brother, Sam, wasn't as scared of them as he had been when they'd lived on the station.

The cyborgs had all been big men before, but with the enhancements they had undergone, they were *huge,* now. Stronger than any normal person. Faster. Able to make nearly instantaneous calculations with the computers in their brains. It was also pretty clear that they had some kind of open comm channel that connected them. What one knew, they all knew. Or, so it seemed.

The cyborgs had taken anyone brave enough to go with them and were now leading a group of refugees on a path through the Milky Way Galaxy. They couldn't go back to Earth. They also couldn't go anyplace where the human military held sway. The cyborgs had been ordered to defend *Eagle Nest Station* to their deaths. Instead, they'd chosen to help the women and children who'd been abandoned by the military and the elites, and take them to safety.

The alien jit'suku were not known to take prisoners. Commanding the small cyborg contingent on the station to defend it against an overwhelming force was equivalent to handing them their death sentences. Only foolish machines would have followed that order when there were innocent lives at stake, and the cyborgs were nobody's fools.

The women had organized themselves into work parties, and they'd started holding formal gatherings—meetings—with the cyborgs, every few days. Or, more often, if there was something important to discuss. They'd already decided on several courses of action.

They had started a school and Sam was continuing his education while Billie was on the bridge. He'd already made a few friends around his age and if Billie had to work late, she had found that the mothers of his new friends were willing to look after him. The ladies had banded together, for the most part, to help each other, and it felt like they were going out of their way to help her, in particular. She couldn't thank them enough.

The meetings had helped the other women have better access to the cyborgs who ran the ship, though Billie was one of the few who had skills that put her in such close contact with the cyborgs. Several important decisions had already come out of the communal get-togethers. They had made a rather daring excursion to mine the tail of a comet not too long ago. They had needed the ice to replenish their water stores, which had been inadequate for the length of time they expected to be in transit. The result of that dangerous little adventure had netted them a cache of precious metals and other elements with which they could barter for supplies, along with plenty of water.

The women had voted for a small group of representatives to be their official liaisons with the cyborgs. Billie was one of them, since, as co-navigator, she worked so closely with the command group on the bridge. And they'd all decided where to go—which was where Billie's nav skills came in handy.

She had left the most recent meeting only to go to the bridge and plot a course for their agreed-upon destination. The women had decided to let Billie be their spokeswoman to the captain of the ship—an intimidating cyborg called Medeus. Since she was on the bridge almost all the time, that made sense, but it also made her uneasy.

Billie found herself unaccountably attracted to Medeus, despite his scary appearance. Whoever had altered him after his injuries had left him looking more machine than most of the other cyborgs. His face, in particular, had been left with jagged scars where the pseudoskin that covered the repairs joined the original skin.

He'd taken severe damage to the left side of his face. That much was clear. He had an artificial eye on that side, and a diagonal swath of pseudoskin that had not been shaded to match the rest of him. It was an obvious repair that few of the other men showed, even though they'd all had critical damage to be turned into cyborgs.

Medeus had likely been strikingly handsome when he'd been whole. Strong jaw, chiseled lips, which were original, since the scar slashed across the left upper side of his face, from the hairline, between his eyes and downward angling toward his ear. His nose and jaw remained unchanged, and she could easily see he'd been a devastatingly attractive man.

Wavy black hair and bright blue eyes—one of which was now an implanted mechanical eye that could probably spot a fleck of dust from a mile away. But his other eye gave her an idea of what he must have looked like before. Gorgeous.

Billie had found herself thinking inappropriate thoughts about him at the oddest of times. Sometimes, she'd just watch him out of the corner of her eye as he went about his duties on the bridge. She lived in fear of being caught staring at him by one of the observant cyborgs. Her crush on Captain Medeus was nobody's business but her own.

Still, being *assigned* to talk to him on a regular basis was no hardship. So, why was she tingling with anticipation at the idea? He was a cyborg. Newly awakened, unlike some of the others. He'd been struggling only a short time to access his lost humanity. She'd seen him doubt, though not when it came to command of the old freighter.

Billie tended to see Medeus as more human than machine, but she knew that was far from the truth. The captain still had a long way to go in recapturing who he had been, and any woman who pinned her hopes on him was probably setting herself up for a great big fall. Billie knew it in her head, but her heart had other ideas.

Knowing they were in for a wild ride no matter what they found at the human colony they were targeting as their first stop, Billie laid in the course after clearing it with the cyborg next to her. He had been checking her work against his internal computer from the moment she'd been given the seat at the nav station. He wasn't a qualified navigator, but the captain had told her the man in the co-nav position was good with numbers and spatial geometry. He was also able to check her work well enough to keep the cyborg contingent happy that she wasn't plotting a course that would pop them out in the middle of a supernova.

She almost resented it, but she was only a fledgling navigator, with a little more than half her formal education completed. If she'd been on her first real assignment, a senior navigator would be checking her work, she reminded herself. She tried hard not to let her feelings show, but she was fast coming to dislike the young cyborg they'd partnered her with. He was just a little too smugly machine-like for her taste.

"Course laid in," she reported as she completed the input.

"Helmsman, implement new course," Medeus instructed the cyborg at the helm.

As she watched her course start to take hold of the old ship, she crossed her fingers for luck, but it was the captain who surprised her with his quiet words.

"For better or worse, there's no turning back now."

CHAPTER 1

The freighter dubbed the *Tobias Bay* came out of jump space just where Billie had calculated. The captain had asked for a non-standard entry into the target system and Billie had enjoyed the challenge. Most star systems had mapped routes for entry and exit. Space lanes, they were sometimes called. Safe pathways past gravity wells and other hazards that had been plotted and standardized by generations of navigators, and ratified by the Navigators Guild.

All traffic was supposed to adhere to the standard routes, for both safety and convenience, but there was nothing standard about this ship or its mission. Their safety might well lie in stealth and Billie had agreed when the captain had explained why he wanted a different approach to the system. Their lives might very well depend on being able to take a look at the colony from an unexpected angle before they made any overtures.

The *Tobias Bay* wasn't a warship. It couldn't fight its way out of trouble. Though the *Toby* may have been an old ship, she had also been well-maintained over her many years of service. The attention their new Chief Engineer, Roxy, was giving to all systems didn't hurt, either. The old *Toby* was being fixed, system by system, until she was humming happily along.

There were still a few rough spots, but nav wasn't one of them. Billie was glad of that. She was still very new at navigation, but her instructors at the space academy had all said she had a natural feel for it. Some people did. Many didn't. Billie was lucky that the flair for interstellar navigation ran in her family. Both her father and older brother had been military navigators on warships, and both had been lost in battle.

When her mother had died in a freak accident not long after Sam's birth, Billie had been left with few choices. She had lived off her parents' savings for as long as she could while Sam had been small, but once he reached the age where he could go to school, she'd devised a plan to help secure both of their futures. She'd decided to follow in their father and older brother's footsteps and get a navigator's license of her own. Civilian, of course. She took after her mother in that she didn't like fighting. Her mom had been content to leave that up to the men in the family…which, of course, had ultimately meant the end of the family altogether.

"Position?" Captain Medeus's deep voice sounded at her side, much closer than she expected.

He'd walked right up to the nav station again, his silent steps surprising her. How such a big man could move so quietly, she didn't understand, but all the cyborgs were like that. Phantoms. Or ninjas. Yeah, a bunch of mechanical ninjas with bulging muscles.

Damn. She really had to stop thinking such thoughts. She was going to embarrass herself one of these days by saying something inappropriate aloud. She just knew it.

She used her best business tone to give the captain the information he wanted. He followed the star map one of his fellows had thoughtfully put up on the main screen at the front of the bridge. It showed their position relative to the small human colony for which they'd been aiming.

Medeus's hand touched her shoulder, sending tingles down her spine. "Good work, Billie."

"Thanks," she replied, touched by the way he'd taken a moment to compliment her.

He didn't do that with his fellow cyborgs, which either meant he thought she needed the—literal—pat on the back or that he was starting to feel more human with her than with his brethren. She hoped it was the latter. Otherwise, all her dirty fantasies about him would be for naught.

Not that she was intending to act on any of them. She just... She wished he was more comfortable with his humanity. For his sake. He seemed so uncertain, at times. It made her heart go out to him, and that couldn't be good. She didn't want to fall in love with a cyborg. There was no future in it.

Of course, she wasn't sure anybody on this refugee ship had a future at all, considering their circumstances. And with the jits invading again, there could be no future for humanity, as a whole. The war was ramping up again, if what had happened at *Eagle Nest Station* was any indication.

"How far to comm range for the colony?" Medeus asked, moving away, back toward his command chair. He had all the controls at his fingertips from that specially designed station.

"Approximately four hours at present speed and course," Billie answered, having calculated that as soon as her screens cleared.

She'd spent part of the past days in transit researching the colony they were heading for in the ship's historical databases. The old cargo ship didn't have much in its information banks, but it did have some data on commercial interests all over human space. From the ship's records, she learned that the *Toby* had visited the colony twice before over the past twenty years. Each time, they'd successfully traded with the colonists, which boded well for their current mission.

She'd also learned that the Aziner colony had been named for the long-dead financier, Henry Aziner, who had taken a gamble on a mining operation way out on the edge of human-occupied space. It had paid off, but not during the man's lifetime. His heirs did well out of the colony proceeds for a few decades, but then, the war started in earnest, and the colonists declared their independence from Earth and any other government than their own.

They were renegades, but they also supplied the military through several substantial contracts, so they were allowed to go their own way, even though one of old Henry's heirs had tried to take them to court. The cases were indefinitely stalled since Aziner Colony had one of the few highly productive mining operations for a key component in military-grade armor. With the war on, that was more important than some trust-fund baby's claim to a place they'd probably never see and people they didn't care about, other than as a source of potential income.

"No other ships on scan, Captain," one of the cyborgs reported from the scan station. Billie suspected they spoke aloud for her benefit, and to make themselves seem more human, but she knew they had something akin to an open comm line in their brains, over which they could communicate with any other cyborg all over the ship.

"Very well," Medeus replied. "First-shift crew, stand down for three hours. Get something to eat and be back here an hour before contact range."

Billie was glad of the break. She'd been on the nav board for the past four hours straight, nervously awaiting the results of their return to normal space. It was the middle of sleep-shift and Sam was being cared for by the mother of one of his school friends. The timing of their transition back to normal space meant she'd had to catch sleep wherever she could in preparation. She'd had time to plan and had made arrangements for Sam to sleep over with his friend and go to school from there when main-shift began.

Billie was just glad they had come out where she'd calculated. She was gaining confidence with each course she plotted and each successful outcome, but she was still a novice, so she worried about every little detail.

She stood from her seat and stretched her back. The chair wasn't exactly comfortable, but considering she'd almost been left behind on a station about to be overrun by aliens, she couldn't complain. Still, it would feel good to take a short break before the next step on their journey.

Medeus was unable to stop watching the lone human female on the bridge. Billie fascinated him on every level, and when she stood up to stretch, he just about stopped breathing. Her lithe body made his pulse race, and his cock stirred in a way it hadn't since before he'd been turned into a cyborg.

She made him think forbidden thoughts about what it would be like to make love with her. But that could never be. He was a cyborg, now, with more obvious replacement parts than most of his brethren. He was way more machine than man, even if he remembered being the fleet commander that put fear into the hearts of humanity's enemies.

He wasn't Commander Michael Bennet, anymore. No, Michael Bennet had perished long ago, leaving only Medeus behind. A weird amalgam of man and machine that didn't quite know who he was supposed to be. He couldn't expose Billie to the mess of his life or the danger he now posed to everything that was weaker than his cybernetic limbs.

He could so easily crush the life out of her and every fragile female on this tub. He wouldn't take the chance. He'd rather stay celibate than hurt a woman. Especially Billie of the soft voice, worried eyes and nervous twitches, as she watched her calculations with an anxious, but eager expression.

She fascinated him, though. Tall, lithe, with a voice like sweet honey and eyes that followed him. Haunted him. Those hazel brown eyes held the stars that ran in her blood. He didn't want to tell her, but he'd known a navigator named Alex Latimer who had those same hazel eyes and light brown hair. Her older brother, he had no doubt.

Alex had been what was known informally as a natural

nav, like his legendary father before him. They could almost feel their way from one position in space to the next. Alex had been nav first on Medeus's flagship when it went down in a ball of fire. Whether others from his crew had been saved the way he had and turned into cyborgs, he didn't know. There was a small possibility Alex and so many others might be out there, even now, with CCS's controlling their every move. Or, they could be awakening, the way Medeus recently had. Or, they could be dead—either from the original battle or some subsequent dispute somewhere far away.

It was hard to kill a cyborg, but it did happen. Especially since their human commanders saw them as expendable. They were sent into impossible situations where human troopers wouldn't go. Toxic atmospheres. Dangerous conditions. Suicidal missions. That's where you would find cyborg troops being used up by people who saw them as less than men.

Billie didn't need to know any of that. He had decided not to mention that he'd known her older brother. It would only hurt her more. He had no doubt that the military had informed her of Alex's death aboard Medeus's ship. If they'd taken Alex and made him into a cyborg, she would not have been told.

Medeus thought it would be cruel to tell her that he'd been there when her brother had died for a couple of reasons. He didn't want her to get her hopes up that Alex might be out there somewhere, remembering her even now. He also didn't want her to realize that Medeus had been the one giving the orders that had put her brother—and the entire crew—into a situation where the ship would be destroyed. Ultimately, it had been his error in judgment that had killed all those people he'd commanded. Friends, many of them. Innocents, like Alex Latimer.

It was selfish of Medeus, in one respect. He didn't want Billie to think less of him. He didn't want to face her righteous anger over how he had caused the death of her brother. He wanted to forget that life—the instant spark of recognition he'd had when he'd first seen Billie's face that had brought on a torrent of memories of his past. He wanted to focus, instead, on this moment. This mission.

He had to, or he'd drown in regret, anger and despair. He had new responsibilities, now. The other cyborgs and the women and children on this old tub were looking to him to ferry them safely across the sea of stars to someplace where the war wasn't happening and they could live their lives in peace.

To do that, he needed the best performance he could get from his crew, which now included Billie, and a very young Latimer boy who might grow up to be much like Alex. Medeus had to give him that chance. He had to try to ignore the way Billie's unique fragrance wafted straight into his brain every time he stopped beside the nav station and caught a subtle hint of the apple-scented shampoo she used on her hair. Billie must have had it in her duffel when she came aboard because none of the other women he'd come across smelled like his beautiful novice navigator, who showed all the signs of being a brilliant natural nav, just like her older brother.

When he'd been human, Medeus would've enjoyed being with a woman just like her, but he'd been wedded to his job. His ship had been his mistress. A top-of-the-line battle cruiser. The best humanity had ever produced. His crew had been his family. His brothers, sisters, and children. Until it had all blown up in his face…literally.

When he'd been put back on active duty as a cyborg, he'd had no memory of the fleet commander he'd once been, but he remembered now. Each memory hurt as it came to life. Memories of a past he could never recapture and people he had lost forever. Not to mention his flagship.

The *Vanguard* had been a fierce piece of machinery with a heart that beat in a thousand chests. Each member of the crew was that heartbeat and their actions the ship's life-blood. The *Vanguard* was in a billion tiny pieces now, somewhere in uncharted space. A navigation hazard to all who dared cross the debris field that had once been a noble ship of the line.

Remembering the *Vanguard* and then realizing he was now the captain of a ship considerably less glorious than his old flagship hurt in a different way. The *Tobias Bay* had never been a warship. She was old and slow, with no weaponry to speak of, but at least she was sound. And, with Chief Engineer Roxy's tender care, the ship's drives were in better shape than they had been in years.

If nothing else, she was a ship, in space. Where Medeus had always felt most comfortable. If he was going to die, he'd often thought, let it be on the bridge of a ship under his command. He'd almost done it once, when the *Vanguard* went down in a blaze of glory, but they'd brought him back. Sometimes, he wished they'd let him die with his flagship, but those weren't the cards he'd been dealt.

He would have to play the hand he'd been given and make the best of it. At least he could help some innocent people along the way. Leaving all those civilians on the station to perish just wasn't right. He'd captain any sort of ship, as long as it had the ability to protect the people now living on the *Tobias Bay* and making it their home.

Billie took a few moments to go back to the suite she shared with her little brother and freshen up a bit. The suite consisted of a main room that they shared, with two smaller bedrooms opening off the main cabin, and a small lav they had all to themselves. There were a few of these family-style suites onboard. The crew of the old freighter must have had many families with children at one time.

The cyborgs were still working on putting in more partitions in the crew areas so that every child could live in a suite like this. Billie had been lucky to get one of the ready-made suites because she worked on the bridge and might need the monitoring capabilities Sam's room had built in, should she ever need to go to work while Sam was sleeping or otherwise unsupervised.

She could turn on full monitoring of his room and be

alerted to any changes in his sleep pattern, or if he woke up. There were medical monitors that gauged his temperature and heart rate, among other things. If he got sick, she would know immediately. She could also communicate with him directly over a comm line that fed right into his bedroom and reassure him from wherever she was on the ship. He was old enough to utilize this kind of system now, and the cyborgs had made sure Billie was comfortable with it so that she could do her job as navigator at any time, during any shift.

Mostly, though, Billie made prior arrangements with one of the other women to keep an eye on Sam, along with their own children. Sam had a few friends who were also quartered in the family cabins and there was room for him to sleepover on occasion. The kids enjoyed having sleepovers so they could stay up late playing games on the entertainment system, and the parents indulged them. Their recent circumstances had been tough on the kids and it helped the parents to see them happy.

Sam was in school at the moment, so Billie was able to stretch out on the couch and shut her eyes for a few moments. Her thoughts raced, though, and she was unable to truly rest. She gave up after a few minutes and spent some time tidying the cabin before giving up and heading out to the dining hall. She grabbed a cup of coffee and a snack, sitting by herself and reviewing data on her tab for a while before it came time to head back to the bridge.

She felt better for the break, but she was also eager to see what they would discover about the colony. Medeus had asked for a very cautious approach and Billie was curious to see what they would learn. She headed back to the bridge with quick steps, entering to find everyone else seemed to have the same intrigued light in their eyes as she took her place at the nav station.

Exactly three hours after he'd given the order, the main-shift crew was back at their posts. Medeus hadn't left the bridge with the others. His biological systems were secondary to the mechanical parts that had replaced a good portion of his original body. He didn't have to rest as much as the others because he was less flesh and blood than almost any cyborg he knew.

Besides which, he felt at home on the bridge, in the command chair. He felt at ease in a way he didn't feel anywhere else. He spent most of his time there now, since taking the *Tobias Bay* out from the station. As he remembered his former life, the familiar feel of being in command of a ship seemed to steady him…even if it wasn't a warship.

"Captain," the cyborg on the comms board sought Medeus's attention, "the civilian leadership has signaled that they are on their way up to the bridge."

"Let them in," he said to Ajax, who was beside the locked hatch.

They were about to implement a plan they had devised on how best to approach the human colony. The women would be the ones to make contact, and the cyborgs would keep their presence aboard hidden as best they could. To that end, the leaders the women had elected would take visible positions on the bridge, as if they were running the ship.

A few moments later, the women arrived. Ajax had the hatch open even before they reached it and shut it behind them. Even on a ship such as this, Medeus had stressed to his brethren that security procedures would be followed. That included keeping the bridge locked down at all times.

Medeus stood from his command chair and reluctantly turned it over to Cordelia. She had been an administrator on the station, and it was agreed that she had the required command presence to pass herself off as captain of the *Toby*. Billie and Roxy would maintain their positions as navigator and chief engineer to round out the scene. The cyborgs would position themselves behind the floating cam that would show only the three women during this first contact.

"How close are we?" Cordelia asked, a bit of her nervousness showing in the way her hands fluttered for a moment before she got them under control.

"We've got about five minutes before we should start broadcasting," Billie answered. "You know what you're going to say?"

Cordelia nodded. "I've got the first part memorized. What comes next will depend on what kind of answer we get."

"Sounds like a plan, Captain." Billie winked at her as Cordelia jumped a bit at the title. "Better get used to it. You're on in four minutes."

"Any words of advice?" Cordelia asked Medeus before he left the area of the command chair.

"Just relax. And don't push any buttons. I've locked out most of the controls, but there are a few things—that first row up there in particular—that cannot be bypassed easily." He pointed to the controls in question on the right side of his chair, which Cordelia now occupied.

She looked aghast but soon got her expression under control. "I'll remember," she promised. "They don't launch weapons or anything like that, right?"

Medeus had to smile. "We don't have any weapons," he told her. "We're a cargo vessel, remember?"

He wouldn't disclose the weapons his men had been working to build in two of the smaller cargo bays. They weren't ready yet, for one thing, and would be of limited usefulness until they got certain key parts.

"Almost show time," Billie reminded them all. "Two minutes."

"I'll be right over there if you need me," Medeus told the nervous woman in his chair.

He tried to inject some confidence into his tone, but he wasn't very good at such subtleties yet. His memories of being human had only just started to come back, and he still didn't remember a lot of things.

Medeus went to stand with the other cyborgs, out of camera range. For the next few minutes, their fates rested in the hands of the women. He just wished Cordelia didn't look so nervous.

"Whenever you're ready, point at me, and I'll start the

transmission," said Jason, the cyborg who was manning the comm panel, out of sight of the floating cam he'd be controlling.

Cordelia straightened her top and smoothed her hair. As Medeus watched, she seemed to get a hold of herself, and the nervous twitches stopped. Good. She cleared her throat, looked down, then pointed at Jason. He pointed back when the cam went live and the little light on top of the floater started flashing, then went to a steady red.

"Aziner Colony Control, this is the cargo vessel *Tobias Bay*, Captain Cordelia Renquist commanding. Are you receiving? Over." To the comm station off screen, Cordelia gave the command to repeat her message at five-minute intervals for the benefit of anyone who might be watching, then cut the feed with a slicing motion of her hand. The cam went into standby mode, the light on top blinking.

The old-fashioned language had been standard throughout human space for initiating contact since the discovery of radio. Medeus had helped Cordelia with her script, and even he had to admit, she delivered her lines very convincingly. She didn't look nervous at all, now.

She sighed. "And now, we wait."

They'd all decided to stay where they were so as not to be caught out if the colony answered right away. The cyborgs stayed on their side of the cam, and the ladies sat quietly, Roxy and Billie watching instruments while Cordelia just sat, not touching anything.

The reply from the colony control center came on the third repeat of the initial broadcast.

"*Tobias Bay*, this is Aziner Colony Control. You're not on our schedule. What brings you here?" The reply was voice only, no corresponding image, but that wasn't uncommon for initial contacts.

They'd planned what to say in answer to this query during their transit. Best to stick with some truth...just not all of it.

"Our ship put in for repair at *Eagle Nest Station* just before a jit invasion force came through the jump point. They let civilians evacuate, so we went," Cordelia replied.

"So, you're running empty?" the person manning the control center asked.

"No, we have cargo and commodities to trade. We're just not on our scheduled route. We decided to stay away from potential danger zones for a bit, just in case this is a full-scale invasion. Have you any news?" Cordelia asked, injecting just the right amount of concern into her voice.

The forward screen flickered to life as the colony control center added an image to their transmission. An older woman's face filled the screen. She had shrewd eyes that were narrowed in thought as she replied.

"Go ahead and send your manifest of trade goods and what you want in return. We haven't had a ship through in a while, and we're always willing to trade if you have things we want. As for the rest... We've only heard bits and pieces. *Eagle Nest* and a few other outlying stations were overrun, but the larger stations are holding out, last we heard. There have been a few space battles, but humanity seems to be holding its own, inflicting as much damage on the enemy as possible. The jits might have those secondary stations, but they're not gaining much more ground than that, and we think those stations will be either destroyed or reclaimed until the jits are pushed back out of the galaxy. At least, that's what the news vids say. But we're a backwater, and we don't get a real-time feed, so our news is a few days old."

"That's good enough for me," Cordelia said. "We hadn't heard anything since fleeing the station." She pointed to off camera for effect. "We're sending through the manifest, now," she told the controller. "We're on approach to dock with your orbital station. ETA roughly seventy hours. I can get a closer estimate if you let us know where you want us to dock."

"I'll call up to the station and confer. One of us will be back in touch in about an hour. Aziner Control out." The forward screen blanked as the transmission cut.

Cordelia let out a breath. "I think that went well."

Medeus couldn't argue with her assessment. He sent the floating cam back to its storage area with a silent command over his computer link to the ship, then walked over to his command chair. "You did very well, ma'am," he said politely. "You can take a quick break if you want but stand ready in case they call back."

"Understood, Captain. I'll just go freshen up, then I'll come right back. I'm not really used to this kind of pressure, anymore," she told him, shaking her head.

"You did fine." He tried to sound reassuring as she stood from his chair and headed for the exit.

He noticed her hands trembling, again, and silently communicated with Aristaeus, one of his cyborg brethren who had been a chaplain before his cyborganization. Aristaeus had been working closely with the human women, helping them make the ship more livable. He might be of some help in calming Cordelia down.

CHAPTER 2

Medeus reclaimed the command chair with a sense of satisfaction. He would have to give it up again, of course, but he was humble enough to admit—if only to himself—that he felt more comfortable in that chair than anyplace else in the universe. It didn't really matter that it was an old, dilapidated command chair. It was the nerve center of the ship, and right now, *any* ship made Medeus feel more at home. Even an old cargo hauler.

Everything about his life—*his* former life—had almost been erased. Subsumed by the CCS implanted in his head. He shuddered to think that he had almost lost everything about himself. Everything that made him the man he had been. The unique individual, different from the other cyborgs, not just one in a very long line of men who had been repaired against their will.

All cyborgs were supposed to be interchangeable. They had different parts depending on their original injuries and the needs of the service at the time they were rebuilt, but essentially, they were just machines—one very much like the other. But, of all the cyborgs on the ship, Medeus was the only one who had been a fleet commander.

There were others of higher rank, of course, but those had been among the ground troops. There were three pilots, who now occupied the helm station in rotation. There were others who had been on ships in varying capacities. But only one fleet commander. Only one who remembered how it had been to be in charge of not only his warship, but an entire fleet of them.

Medeus knew he would never command a fleet, again. For now, just having this one ship under his control steadied him. It gave him comfort, when there was little to be had in the situation. Everything he had ever known had been wiped away, but it was starting to come back to him in brief glimpses, and being on the bridge, in the chair, made it possible to retain most of his equilibrium. Without the command chair to prop him up, he was very much afraid he'd be a blubbering mess over what had been done to him as the memories came flooding back.

It had already been decided that Cordelia would lead a small delegation that would leave the ship when they docked at the orbital station. Billie and Roxy were going with her for the first contact. Other women would be allowed to leave the ship to conduct trading business, once it was deemed safe. They were also going to let others leave the ship altogether, if they wished, but that would be the last group to go, once trading had been concluded.

They wouldn't leave anyone in the lurch, but by the same token, they had agreed it would be bad for business if any truly unhappy folks started badmouthing the ship and its crew before they'd attained the trade goods they needed. The welfare of the ship had to come first because the vast majority of those aboard wanted to keep going with the cyborgs, who they believed could keep them safer than anyone else if the war was truly on again all over the galaxy.

A few had felt strongly about checking out the colony and leaving if it looked at all hospitable. Mostly, it was a few mothers with young children, who wanted a more stable environment for their offspring.

Personally, Billie had decided that she and Sam would stay with the ship. She was a navigator. Or, at least, she was halfway to her professional certification. She had dreamed of being where she was now—at the nav station of a ship. Any kind of ship. She wouldn't trade this experience for anything, and she also believed—like many others—that the cyborgs were the best companions to have in these uncertain times. She truly believed that Sam and she had a better chance of survival in this time of war if they were with the cyborgs.

The fact that they were remembering who they had been only made her feel safer with them. If any place could be truly safe with the jits on the prowl once more. The cyborgs were at least human. Or, they had been. They remembered their former lives, and that made her feel both more secure with them and sorry for them. She knew they carried heavy emotional burdens, but none of them seemed to let that get in the way of the task at hand. Namely, protecting civilians aboard and finding refuge for them.

Billie walked slightly behind Cordelia, letting her lead the way out of the ship, into the docking area. Cordelia was supposed to be the captain, after all. Billie and Roxy walked side by side, after her.

There was a delegation made up mostly of women, surprisingly, waiting for them. The older, gray-haired woman they had spoken to over the comm seemed to be in charge, leading the small delegation. There was also a younger woman who looked enough like the old lady to be her granddaughter, and a young male who looked like he wasn't old enough to shave, yet.

"I'm Amelia Aziner," the old woman announced, making Billie start a little, though she did her best to hide her reaction. "My granddaughter, Elizabeth, and grandson, Bartholomeu."

Cordelia nodded respectfully. "Cordelia Renquist," she replied smartly. "And this is Billie Latimer and Roxanne

Abernathy. Thank you for meeting with us."

"I'm duty bound to inform you that no one else will be allowed to leave your ship until we've established rules for your visit, and your identities. We also want to hear your story about *Eagle Nest Station*. Perhaps we could adjourn to the lounge…" Amelia gestured toward a grouping of soft chairs and a sofa behind a transparent wall off to one side of the dock access.

"By all means," Cordelia agreed, walking with Amelia toward the doorway that slid aside at their approach.

Billie followed, with Roxy beside her, though she noticed a few well-armed security people—again, mostly women and very young men—standing guard immediately outside the dockside access area.

They arrived in the lounge, and Amelia went to a small desk that pushed out from one wall. "Let's get the formalities out of the way first. We'll do the identity checks here, and then we can get down to business."

"Certainly," Cordelia replied with a businesslike smile as she presented her arm, with its implanted identity chip, to the scanner.

Amelia watched the results come up on her screen and nodded. "Cordelia Renquist." She nodded. "You were very high up in the admin of the station," Amelia said, sounding impressed. "Why'd they leave you behind?"

"I objected when the administrators bailed out, fully intending to leave a large percentage of the human population behind, to fend for themselves." Cordelia shrugged and moved aside for Roxy to offer her indent chip.

Amelia hummed over Roxanne's record. She had been a chief engineer and drives mechanic for a while, and that was all in her permanent record, which every citizen carried around on the chip implanted at birth and upgraded many times over the years as they grew. New data was added to the ident chips by stations like this one. In fact, this station would be adding their stop at Aziner Colony to their permanent records, as well. The ident chip was used for medical records, travel documentation, criminal notations, legal proceedings, and a host of other things.

"This doesn't list you as chief engineer of the *Tobias Bay*," Amelia mused as she perused Roxy's identity.

"It's a new position, and it wasn't attained in the regular way," Roxy said with an ironic grin.

"I suppose not," Amelia allowed as Roxy moved away for Billie's turn.

Billie placed her arm under the scanner and waited.

"You're not licensed yet, are you?" Amelia commented as Billie shrugged.

"I was halfway through my formal training. The academy ship took off without me and my little brother." It was no less than the truth. Billie had been abandoned by those she had trusted with her education. "But I come from a nav family. My dad and brother were both military navigators. I learned more from them than I did from the academy."

Amelia nodded. "We value family knowledge here," she said. Billie really didn't know what she meant, but the fact that she was accompanied by her grandson and granddaughter might have something to do with it.

Amelia shut off the scanner and allowed the small device and its little desk to withdraw back into the wall. She then moved to take her seat, facing the three women from the ship.

"We are a small colony," Amelia began. "We are definitely interested in trade, based on the manifest you sent ahead."

"That's good to hear," Cordelia began, but Amelia held up one hand to forestall her words.

"First, however, I'd like to hear more about how the station was overrun. We haven't heard much, but the reports from the outer systems are troubling."

Billie knew that the cyborgs were busy infiltrating the colony's network even as they spoke, trying to learn as much as they could about the situation in the wider galaxy. Any news the colony had received would soon be in the hands of the cyborgs aboard the *Toby*.

Cordelia spent a few minutes recounting the tale of *Eagle Nest Station's* siege, surrender, and evacuation for the colonists. When she was done, Amelia questioned both Roxy and Billie about what they had seen. When she was satisfied, she sat back and seemed to think for a moment, then she spoke.

"Since you were probably wondering, but too polite to ask, I am a direct descendant of the colony financier. My branch of the family came out later, wanting to be a part of old Henry's dream. It worked out well for us until the slavers started operating in our system."

"Slavers?" Billie can help herself. She was shocked.

Amelia merely nodded. "All the younger folk have been spirited away, leaving only the old and young, and any woman not strong or pretty enough to be of value."

"That's outrageous!" Cordelia said, bristling with indignation on the colonists' behalf.

"It is what it is," Amelia said philosophically. "The first raids took place about two years ago and escalated for a time, then stopped. All our efforts since then have been directed toward survival and preparing, in case they return."

"If there's anything we can do—" Cordelia began, but Amelia waved her off with a tired expression.

"A ship full of women? Refugees? I don't think there's anything you can really do for us, except trade. And we're glad of that. I could wish you had more useful items in your holds—weapons, for example—but we're glad enough for a peaceful visit and the chance to trade with anyone. The slavers, or pirates, or whatever they are, seem to have interdicted the system, and we haven't seen any trade ships since the last raid."

Billie began to get an idea, but they'd have to talk it over first, before she said anything. Surely, the cyborgs could do *something*?

"I see," Cordelia said diplomatically. "For now, perhaps we should just start with trade. We are interested in the standard provisions, though we're all set for water, so that's not an issue at present. Air and food is what we're after, and any trade goods you might have that we could sell on at another port of call. Though, of course, that is secondary to air and food."

Billie knew Cordelia was improvising. They hadn't said anything in their discussions about taking on trade goods. Billie was glad, though. These people needed help almost more than the folks on the *Toby* did. They were sitting ducks if the raiders decided to come back.

What followed was an old-fashioned bargaining session. Cordelia showed her worth as an admin by getting good return for the raw materials and commodities they'd mined from the comet's tail. The three women returned to their ship with subdued hearts. Billie was glad they'd been able to secure a deal to top up their air tanks and fill up the larder, but she wished there was more they could do for those left on the colony.

Late in her sleep period, Billie rose, restless. She checked on Sam, fast asleep in his own small room in the suite they'd been given. She didn't want to wake him, so she looked for a book to occupy her mind. Annoyingly, she'd left her library card—which contained her personal library—in the holding slot of the nav station. Deciding to fetch it, she dressed simply and enabled full monitoring on Sam's cabin so she'd know if he woke or had any sort of problem while she was gone. She then prowled up to the bridge to retrieve her card. She stumbled through the hatch with a nod to the cyborg on security duty.

It was the young man who had chosen the name Phoenix. She'd asked him why and he'd said something about being reborn. He might look younger than most of the other cyborgs, but he had deep thoughts, she had discovered.

"Just want to get something I left on my board," she told him, and he let her in with a small smile.

Phoenix was learning how to be human again, and he was really trying. She had a soft spot for the youth who must've been injured during his first battle. He seemed so much less battle-hardened than all the rest of the cyborgs. In many ways, he reminded her of Sam. He had that same youthful innocence, at times.

The bridge was empty, as she expected while powered down at dock, except... There was a very familiar form sitting in the command chair.

"Medeus," she said, before she thought better of it.

He nodded. "Miss Latimer," he replied politely.

She scrunched up her face at his formal words. "You called me Billie before," she told him, her words incautious this late in the night. The bridge was dark, except for the ambient glow from the screens. "What are you doing up here, anyway? Don't you sleep?"

Medeus let out a soft sigh as he stood. "Rarely," he answered. "I'm finding it...difficult...to assimilate my old memories with my new circumstances."

That made Billie pause as she retrieved her library card from its holding slot. She turned to look at him. "I'm sorry," she said quietly. "Maybe if you talk to someone?"

"I have tried, but it's hard to reveal such intimate thoughts to others of my kind. They seem to be taking these...enhancements...so much better than I am. Of course, they were mostly ground troops, so anything that makes them better fighters is something they can embrace, for the most part." He laughed ruefully, sounding so human, in that moment, that she wanted to reach out to him.

"But you were a ship's captain, right?" Billie asked, moving a little closer on the dark bridge.

"Worse. I was a fleet commander," he admitted. "I went from pilot to captain to commander. I never fought hand-to-hand," he admitted. "Maybe that's why I'm finding it so hard to accept."

"Yes, that probably has a lot to do with it," she allowed. "But... Forgive me for saying this if it makes you uncomfortable, but you also seem to be a lot more...uh...enhanced than the others. Maybe that's bothering you, as well?"

Medeus shook his head, looking down at the deck. "You're right, Billie."

Her name on his lips made her spine tingle in a good way. She didn't like it when he got all formal with her. She much preferred when he called her by name. She took another step closer until she was only a foot or so from him.

"I was pretty much blown apart with my flagship. Only the command chair's life pod functions saved me." He paused and looked up, his eyes bright in the darkness of the bridge. "Sometimes, I wish it hadn't."

She couldn't stand it. She had to touch him. She reached out with one hand, placing it on his arm. Metal under synthetic skin. Cyborg. But also a man. A man with feelings that were in a jumble of pain and regret. He might be made of replacement parts, but he had a heart and a mind and a soul. A soul that reached out to hers, as hers reached out to him.

"Don't say that," she told him softly. "Don't ever say that. I, for one, am glad you're here. My life would have been sadder for not knowing you."

"Billie... I'm only just starting to remember things about who I was," he warned her.

"And that's why it's so hard right now, I'd bet. Give yourself some time, Captain. Cut yourself a little slack. You're only human," she said, smiling.

"Not quite human," he reminded her with a shake of his head, though a grin played around the corner of his mouth, giving her hope.

"Human enough," she told him in no uncertain terms. She stepped closer. "Tell me..." She moved his arm out to the side so she could press her body against his. "Would a machine be able to feel this?"

Daring greatly, she pressed her lips to his in the kiss she'd been craving since almost the first time she had laid eyes on him. She was either making a total fool out of herself or about to ignite a flame that might never be quenched. Either way, she was in trouble.

Medeus was shocked right down to his toes when Billie stepped up and kissed him. He thought about it for about zero point two milliseconds before old instincts kicked in, and he kissed her back.

The first kiss since he'd been changed. The first kiss that really *mattered* in a lifetime of regrets. Billie knew what he was and what he'd been through, and still, she kissed him. His human heart filled with wonder, even as his cybernetic limbs moved to embrace her as gently as they possibly could.

He never wanted to hurt this beautiful soul. It would kill him if he misjudged and gave her the slightest bruise. He'd have to be careful with the privilege she'd given him. The privilege of her kiss. Her warmth. Her trust.

Her mouth was warm and inviting, as was her body. He could feel her against him, thanks to the sensors in his limbs—in the pseudo-skin they'd used to craft his replacement parts and make them as responsive as his old body. The only difference between the sensitivity of his new limbs and the old was that he could selectively turn off the sensors in his limbs if he was injured. He could essentially ignore things that would have been intensely painful in a totally biological body.

Medeus supposed that was useful for ground troops. And, while he'd been deployed as a cyborg without memory, he'd done his share of fighting. He'd used the ability to turn off pain receptors. But he would never—not in a billion years—turn off the signals that allowed him to feel the delicious heat and pressure of Billie's lithe body rubbing against him.

He'd never committed to a woman. He'd regretted that, sometimes, when he stopped to think about it. But, really, he'd had no time. His career had been his focus. He'd always figured a wife and children would come later. Maybe.

And then, time had run out for him.

He'd floated in the nothingness of the CCS dominance over his brain for a long time, and then, he'd awakened to this new reality. A reality where he could be a shadow of the man he'd once been… And a woman he'd never expected was suddenly in his arms, kissing him as if he mattered. Really *mattered*.

His all-too-human heart stuttered at the enormity of the moment. Billie was a smart, beautiful young woman with her whole life ahead of her. Why would she be drawn to the wreck—both physical and emotional—that he was?

Medeus knew he should be pushing her away, but he couldn't help but wring every last moment of enjoyment he could out of the experience. Before he had to put her aside and do something to deter her from further intimacy.

There was too much that she didn't know about who he had been. Too much he couldn't tell her for fear of hurting her more. Her older brother had been one of his officers and had likely died under his command. That was too big an obstacle to surmount.

His mind knew it couldn't work between them, but that didn't mean his body got the message. He kissed her with all the pent-up longing inside him until he didn't know where he left off and she began. And then… It was over. She pulled away, breathing heavily, and he let her go.

He stepped back once he knew she was steady on her feet. Her eyes were dazed, and a primitive part of him liked that he'd been able to put that look on her pretty face. The saner side of him knew he had to nip this in the bud before it could go any further.

"I'm sorry," he said quietly, but firmly. "I shouldn't have done that."

Confusion shone in those pretty eyes. Confusion, embarrassment, and a bit of hurt. He felt bad about it, but it couldn't be helped. She'd be hurt a lot worse if he let this continue.

"Go back to your cabin, Billie." He could, at least, give her the courtesy of calling her by name, now that he'd kissed her. He wouldn't be so cruel as to take that away, as well.

Medeus turned away, cursing himself as every kind of fool, unable to look at her tragic expression. He didn't watch, but he was well aware when she padded quietly to the hatch and opened it, letting herself out. He heard the subdued greeting she gave the young cyborg he'd stationed outside before the hatch closed and locked behind her.

Medeus was alone, once again.

CHAPTER 3

Billie was glad she didn't have to spend any time on the bridge while they were docked. After that midnight encounter, she didn't really want to see Medeus anytime soon. She'd been absolutely floored by his kiss. Devastated. Demolished.

And then, he'd turned away. It had felt like a slap in the face. A cruel dismissal. She'd been hiding, licking her wounds, for the rest of the night. Oh, she knew she'd have to see him eventually, but she'd happily wait a day or two.

Unfortunately, she couldn't wait as long as she'd hoped. Cordelia called a ship-wide breakfast meeting that next morning, to discuss what they'd learned from Amelia and what they should do—if anything—about it. Cordelia had discussed the things they'd learned with Chiron and Medeus, Billie knew, as soon as they'd returned from speaking with Amelia.

She supposed they'd decided that the issue was too big to make a quick decision on their own and had opted to put it before everyone. The message about the meeting was waiting on her cabin comm when she woke, and she had only a half hour to get Sam to the schoolroom and make herself presentable before the gathering.

Medeus would be there, she was certain. She wasn't sure if she was ready to face him, but it looked like she had little choice. Squaring her shoulders, she entered the mess hall—the only room big enough to accommodate all the adults aboard. She took a seat near the rear of the group, as far from where she figured Medeus would stand as possible.

When the captain arrived a few minutes later, along with his contingent of cyborgs, she watched them line themselves up along the walls of the big room, allowing the human refugees to take the seats at the tables in the center. Medeus stood at the center of the cyborg line, with Chiron and a few others who were leaders among the cyborgs.

Cordelia stood up front, as well. She was the first to speak, revealing what they had learned from the colony spokeswoman to everyone.

"We've ironed out some trade deals. The food we requested is already being moved up from the surface to the orbital station for our inspection later today. As soon as we approve the rations, we can begin transferring payment to the colonists while the air tanks are being topped up from station supplies. That was the agreement," Cordelia told them. "What we need to decide is what to do next. I know some of you were hoping to get off the ship here and stay with the colony. After learning about the slavers' raids, I decided you all needed to know about the colony's situation before you could make your decisions. Plus, the captain and his people have learned a bit more about the galactic situation that I think we all need to hear. Captain?"

Cordelia turned the floor over to Medeus. He stepped forward, nodding politely to her, his expression dark and unreadable. Billie's heart skipped a beat when he met her gaze, but the moment was too fast for anyone else to notice, thank goodness. She didn't want everyone aboard knowing that she was ga-ga over the captain. Especially with the way he'd shut her down last night. It would just be too embarrassing.

"We have been combing through the news feeds and archives of the colony," Medeus said without preamble. "What happened at *Eagle Nest* was not an isolated incident. Several other outlying stations near smaller jump points were also overrun around the same time. Our analysis indicates a concerted effort by the enemy to ramp up the war once again. It's a massive invasion, the likes of which we have not seen in decades." Murmurs of dismay filled the room, but Medeus didn't let that stop him. "We know a bit about what the military response will be," he said, talking over some of the frightened tones and regaining everyone's attention. "We expect full mobilization of human forces throughout the sectors where jit'suku have already infiltrated, and those that are high value targets."

"What does this mean to us?" one of the women wanted to know. She looked scared, reflecting the thoughts, Billie had no doubt, of many others in the room. "Where can we be safe?"

"That is the question," Medeus said calmly. "We cyborgs have reason to avoid the human military, though many of us are torn. Since we've awakened, our free will has reasserted itself. It would be next to impossible to go back to the way we were—and the way we were treated. Many of us still want to do what we can to protect humanity, but we don't think, at this juncture, that we can accomplish that goal by going backward. Whatever we eventually decide to do, it will have to be something new, where we can exercise our free will like any other human. We won't go back to being treated like machines. We're more than that, now."

Roxy gave a loud "Here, here!" emphasizing her agreement with Medeus's words. Of course, Roxy was in love with Chiron, so her support of the cyborg agenda was more or less expected. Still, Billie felt a lot of compassion for the men who had saved them and now sought to re-make their own lives like phoenixes being reborn from the ashes of their prior existences.

"That being said," Medeus went on, "we will have to be very careful in what course we choose from here. Considering what we've learned here, many of us wish to help the human colony, but we are loath to reveal our presence aboard. We've been discussing ways we could, perhaps, do something from space. For one thing, we could take a closer look around the system and see if there's some reason trade ships have been bypassing the colony. It might be that it's something simple that we could fix, or at least tell the colonists about."

"I like that idea," Cordelia said. "Leaving them in this situation is not my first choice. It's clear they need help, but with the mobilization to fight the jit'suku, I doubt the military can spare anyone to help one distant colony. I think the people on the planet below are pretty much on their own. If we can help in any way, I believe we probably should."

Medeus nodded at Cordelia. "We feel the same. Some of us are better at comms and research than others. We're still looking into it and will communicate anything we discover. If we find anything that the colonists should know, we would ask that you continue to be the public face of the ship. It's probably best that the colonists don't know about us. At least for now."

"Agreed," Cordelia said.

"However, there is something you ladies need to know. A few of the cyborg contingent have been using spare parts to try to assemble weaponry."

Medeus let that verbal bombshell sit there for a moment. It wasn't long before questions rose from the seated women. He answered them as best he could.

"We don't have all the necessary parts, but if there are more chances for barter with the colony, we have prepared a list of things we could use," he said finally, handing a hard copy to Cordelia.

"These are all common items. None of it looks like weapons parts to me," she said after a quick glance.

"Component parts never really look all that dangerous. It's how you put them together," Chiron spoke up for the first time, giving Cordelia a smile that charmed.

"And you can make something that will…work?" Cordelia asked both men.

"I am assured that our brethren can create something akin to a rail gun that can propel mass at high speed toward a target. If we can make more than one—and two are, in fact, underway right now—we might be able to leave one here with the colony, for their own protection," Medeus said, surprising just about everyone in the hall who wasn't a cyborg. "We talked about it, and we're willing to give up one so these people can have at least some kind of protection," he went on, "but we believe they should mount it on the planet. The orbital station is too vulnerable."

"I can see that," Cordelia said, still acting as their spokesperson. She was really good at administrative matters, so the women were content to let her ask the questions. "But I think that would require us to admit to the presence of at least a couple of cyborgs on our ship. I don't think Amelia would be foolish enough to believe that a bunch of refugee women could cobble something like that together."

"I could," Roxy reminded everyone. "But you're probably right. We came in here claiming to be an unarmed cargo ship. If we change our minds about that, we will have to produce a reason. The cyborgs are the best reason I can think of, and I doubt anyone will be surprised that they have weapons expertise and the ability to make a giant gun out of spare parts."

Cordelia's mouth firmed to a straight line. "I don't like it, but I understand where you're coming from. Still, I think we should leave any discussion of weaponry to the very end of our visit here. Let's get our supplies aboard first before we reveal anything that might anger the colonists."

"A wise precaution," Medeus agreed.

"There's one other topic we should discuss," Cordelia told them all. "Some of us thought we might be able to stop here and join the colony. The reverse might also be true. We might encounter colonists who want to join our crew and get away from here. We should probably think about how we might respond to such requests."

The discussion ranged back and forth for some time. The majority decided to address each situation on a case-by-case basis, if anyone wanted to join the ship. It wasn't an ideal solution, but at least they had a policy in place in case anyone from the colony wanted to take their chances with the ship. When that topic finally wound down, one of the women raised a new question.

"Can we at least go onto the station while we're here? The directory lists several shops and restaurants. Most of us still have a currency balance, and we'd like to go shopping."

A chorus of agreement followed this statement. Medeus looked grim, but it was Cordelia who answered.

"Ladies," she said to get them to quiet down, "I'd like to go shopping as much as the rest of you, but we have to lay a few ground rules first. The biggest one being that we all have to agree not to mention the presence of our cyborg friends to anyone on the station." Quiet murmurs passed among the women. "While we might later reveal their presence if the situation warrants it, right now, we cannot know how the colonists will react. Remember what you all thought of cyborgs before they saved us. I'm sure some of you were afraid of them. Some probably thought they were just dangerous machines. We know better now. They're different. They remember who they were."

The muttering stopped. "We don't want to get anyone in trouble," the first woman insisted in a petulant tone. "We just want to go shopping."

"All right," Cordelia said with a sigh, "we'll figure something out. Let's just get our most critical supplies aboard first, then we'll come up with a plan for the rest of it. We're going to start loading supplies today, if all goes well. The cargo handling group we set up will be interacting with the station folk as we load in. We'll see how that goes, and take it from there, all right?"

Grudging sounds of agreement met Cordelia's words, and

the meeting adjourned soon after. Not everyone was happy, but nobody was truly angry, which was all to the good, Billie thought.

Billie went onto the station with Cordelia and Roxy again, when the food rations arrived from the planet and were ready for inspection. As a primarily agricultural colony, the processing plant on Aziner knew how to package food for deep space travel. In fact, much of their trade had been in just such supplies prior to their problems with the raiders.

When Billie, Roxy, and Cordelia had inspected random samples from the pallets of ration packs, they found the food to be of high quality and very fresh. It was all that the women of the *Tobias Bay* could hope for. The deal was quickly ratified, and goods started changing hands. The women of the *Toby* were busy in the cargo area, loading in the food rations and loading out the items the colonists had wanted in return.

Roxy went to the air supply section and began topping off the tanks that held emergency reserves, connecting to the station supply. Air, food, and water were standard resupply items, which almost all orbital stations could provide. The only thing the *Toby* didn't need, right now, was water. They'd mined enough from the comet's tail to fill up the system, and from there on, it was a matter of the recycling tanks doing their duty. The *Toby* wouldn't need to top up their water supplies again for quite some time.

The colonists were happy to take the base metals the ship's crew had mined from the comet. Their factories were particularly interested in some of the elements they had isolated that could be used to make specialty alloys. They also took a small amount of the precious metals in payment. Those, Amelia had confided, would be squirreled away where raiders would never find them and used as a rainy-day fund for bartering with other visitors. Gold, platinum, and especially iridium, were always considered as hard currency in trade since they were such useful metals. Other elements had lower values but still traded well in many places.

As the ship filled, Billie started to breathe easier. She, like many of the women aboard the *Toby*, had been worried by the state of their supplies. Food, especially, was something they couldn't do without and weren't quite ready to grow themselves. Part of the list Cordelia was haggling for were parts for the old hydroponic system they'd found in one of the larger cargo holds that looked like it hadn't been used in decades.

Most cargo ships on quick runs didn't bother growing their own food since they could pick up supplies wherever they traded. Apparently, the *Toby* had once been used for long-haul transits and had a 'ponics system, but it hadn't been used in a very long time. There was no reason, Roxy assured them, that the old system couldn't be put back into use with a good clean, a fresh injection of nutrients, and the all-important seed stock.

One entire cargo hold was filled with food packs by the end of main-day shift that first full day on station. That's when Cordelia started making further inquiries—the 'ponics components among them. She was able to arrange for nutrient packs and seed stock, though the nutrient packs were a bit old, so they had gotten them at a bit of a discount. Roxy said they would still work but might have lost a bit of their potency.

The newly appointed gardeners would have to monitor the water chemistry closely to start. Oddly enough, a few of the cyborgs had readily volunteered to work on the 'ponics team along with a large number of the women and a few of the older children. The cyborgs would be able to deal with the complicated chemistry using the computers in their brains, which would make the start up of the whole system a lot easier.

Those items started coming aboard during the next main-shift, their second full day on station. They had put aside space in one of the holds for the 'ponics, and the team started to work right away setting things up. None of the women had been allowed out to shop yet, and they were growing restless. After the 'ponics components were delivered and safely in their hold, Cordelia convinced Chiron and Medeus that keeping the women cooped up on board any longer might start a riot. The cyborgs acquiesced, and shopping commenced.

Billie knew all this because, while the women were preparing for their shopping sprees, Medeus had quietly contacted the entire bridge crew, herself included. He'd asked them all to take their places on the bridge just in case a fast departure should become necessary. She'd quickly made arrangements with Sam's teacher and Sheila, the mother of one of Sam's little friends, to watch him after school, should Billie be unable to get away from the bridge.

Billie felt a little odd, sitting in her nav station with Medeus seated in his command chair behind her. She'd been thinking about their kiss ever since it happened, and she felt nervous about dealing with him again. She didn't want to make an even bigger fool out of herself by letting on how much his kiss had really meant to her. She tried to play it cool and just be as professional as possible.

She thought she was succeeding until he snuck up on her again. Without warning, the captain was suddenly at her side, speaking to her in a low, intimate tone.

"I'd like you to plot a course toward the delta quadrant of this system," he told her. "If we need to leave in a hurry, I'd like to be sure that we have plans in place for where to go."

"Yes, sir," she replied respectfully. She turned to her calculations with some relief, as Medeus left her to it.

Billie had just finished plotting her course and turned to Medeus for his approval when Cordelia arrived on the bridge unexpectedly, her expression troubled. Medeus's lips firmed into a thin line. Billie could guess what was about to happen, and she was glad Medeus had taken precautions.

"I'm sorry, Captain," Cordelia began. "You were right to be cautious. Someone has been spreading tales about you and your brethren, and Amelia Aziner is at the hatch, demanding to know if it's true that there are cyborgs on this ship. I told her to wait, but I'm not sure how long she'll be patient."

Medeus shook his head slightly before releasing a small sigh. He looked up, meeting the problem head on, which Billie admired about him. He was such a strong man. A strong leader. But this amounted to a betrayal of him and every cyborg who had risked their own safety to take every last refugee aboard this old freighter.

Billie's heart went out to him, but she couldn't say anything with everyone looking on. She just hoped, somehow, Medeus would know that she felt for him. And that she was very disappointed in the women they'd spent all this time and effort saving. Apparently, not everyone was as honest as she'd thought.

"We planned for this," Medeus told Cordelia. "Chiron will be our representative. We thought his bond with Roxy and her obvious feelings for him might help others see us as closer to human than to machine. At least, that's the theory."

Cordelia nodded slowly. "That's very astute, Captain. I've seen them together, and there is no doubt of the depth of feeling between those two."

"Maybe this is better, in a way," he went on, somewhat fatalistically. "At least now, we'll know where we stand, and if they're the least bit accepting, we could begin talks about the rail gun. I hate to leave so many civilians without any sort of defense."

Billie's heart warmed. Even without knowing how the colonists would react to the cyborg presence, Medeus's thoughts were on their defense. He was not just a good man. He was a *great* man. If humans survived to write history books after this latest jit'suku invasion, Billie thought they should devote an entire chapter to the man who had been a fleet commander and, even through his cyborganization, had never lost sight of his true goal—protecting the innocent.

And, as she thought about his reaction, Billie fell just a little bit more in love with him.

CHAPTER 4

Chiron's meeting with Amelia Aziner went about as well as could be expected. Roxy had gone along with the group, defending Chiron vociferously when Amelia had, at first, tried to treat Chiron like a machine. They'd eventually sat down all together, in the dockside lounge area they'd used before, but Chiron refused to provide his ident chip for their scanner, and Roxy backed him up. Billie suspected that with Chiron present, all the cyborgs still in the ship had a direct line to whatever happened. He was probably getting advice from his brethren as they went along.

"I don't understand why you didn't tell us you had cyborgs aboard when we first discussed the raiders. They could help us." Amelia Aziner sounded mad, but Billie wasn't impressed.

"I don't know what you've heard, but the cyborgs who rescued us when the station was overrun aren't what we were all led to believe. They remember, Amelia." Roxy spoke with clear emotion in her voice. "They may have been more machinelike at first, but their brains have overcome the implants, somehow, and they remember who they were. The *men* they were—and are again."

"Ridiculous," one of Amelia's companions scoffed. She'd brought more than just her grandkids to this meeting as a show of force, Billie reasoned, but it wasn't really working. Chiron was bigger and more badass than any of the callow youths Amelia had acting as her backup.

"Cyborg," Amelia Aziner addressed Chiron while Billie bristled at the condescending, disrespectful tone. "Do you really expect me to believe you can think and act on your own? I've seen what neural implantation does to a brain."

"I wasn't a doctor, ma'am," Chiron replied, his sitting pose as human as he could make it, considering the mechanical limbs he sported. "All I know is that we've been waking up. I was one of the first men modified in our group, and I woke first. I remember my life before. I remember my family, my friends, my education and my career until the point where I was nearly killed. Then, there's a blank when I believe my actions were totally under the control of the implanted computers in my brain. And then, slowly, I started to become more aware of my surroundings, a little at a time, until I realized what had been done to me and where I was."

"Where were you when this process supposedly started?" Amelia still sounded skeptical, but a little more willing to listen.

"The first flash of awareness came when I was being ordered to shoot a child," he admitted, grimacing.

A few of the people with Amelia gasped. The old lady looked a bit aghast, as well. "Surely not. The human military doesn't commit atrocities."

Chiron sighed and rubbed one hand over his jaw. "Have you heard of the Pollander Two Uprising?"

Billie got a sick feeling in her stomach. The news vids had been full of horrible scenes from the far-flung outpost where civilians had tried to stage a revolt against the colonial government and their brutal labor conditions. Due to the rich resources of the planet and its strategic placement in the galaxy, the government back on Earth had sent in troops to *stabilize* the situation.

"My platoon was under the command of Major Manachi. His idea of keeping the peace was to kill everyone in the rebel camp, including the non-combatants—the injured, old people, and mothers with children."

Billie recognized the name of the officer. He'd been tried for war crimes later, when evidence of his butchery had leaked out, somehow.

"I remember seeing shocking body-cam footage on the news," Amelia allowed, her words coming slower now, less accusatory.

"That was mine," Chiron admitted. "When he ordered us to shoot the children, I…" His expression was pained. "I couldn't. He didn't realize it because the rest of my platoon was still under the compulsion of the computers in their brains. They mowed down those kids, and I had to watch," he said, his voice filled with palpable pain. He paused a moment, then cleared his throat and went on. "Mercifully, the next command given, after the massacre, seemed to reboot my system, and I went back under. But I recorded the whole thing over my optical implant. During another lucid moment, I hacked into a news server and uploaded the footage before we left orbit. Thankfully, nobody ever traced the leak to me, but the news got out, and Manachi was punished. Others weren't." He looked grim. "After that, the waking moments came more often until I was completely self-aware again, and aboard *Eagle Nest Station*. I recognized the signs when others of the cyborg contingent there started overcoming their programming and was able to help them hide it from our commanders."

"Are all of you…awake now?" Amelia asked tentatively.

"To different degrees, but yes. We all remember who we were, and we're striving to reconcile that with what we've become," he told her honestly.

"What was your name?" Amelia asked, her eyes taking on a shrewd light.

"Sorry, ma'am. You won't get that out of me. As far as I'm concerned, my former identity is dead and gone. It's easier that way." He didn't explain why, but Billie assumed he'd left family behind back on Earth. "My name is Chiron, now."

Amelia cocked her head as if thinking. "Like the ancient Greek teacher of heroes?"

"I loved mythology as a young man. I studied the classics in school. When I ended up in the role of guide to the others, it seemed a good fit. I'm just a soldier. The rest... They're the real heroes."

Roxy reached out to her man, wrapping her hand around his upper arm and snuggling close. Amelia followed the motion with alert eyes. She seemed to finally realize that the machine sitting before her wasn't *just* a machine. That's when the real bargaining started.

They relayed the results of their meeting at another of the ship-wide gatherings after dinner that night. They had eaten fresh produce bought from the station after many of the women had returned triumphant from their shopping expeditions. Everyone was feeling somewhat mellow when the meeting began, but they didn't stay that way for long.

They waited until the younger children—Sam among them—had been taken off to a play area before starting. Cordelia looked around the room with disappointment in her gaze, and people started to perk up and question what this impromptu meeting was all about. They didn't have to wait long to find out.

"I'm glad you all had fun shopping," Cordelia began. "The thing is... A few of your fellow travelers abused the privilege and the trust we placed in them. You may notice that Ms. Willow and Mrs. Longfellow and their children are no longer in their quarters, and in fact, they are no longer on the ship, at all. They will not be coming back. While it is true they both expressed a desire to stay on the colony, even before we got here and found out what was going on, they had also promised not to reveal the presence of our cyborg friends. Unfortunately, they lied."

Gasps and expressions of disbelief and worry shone

around the room. Cordelia waited for the murmuring to die down before continuing.

"We received some rather accusatory communications from station management and colony control and had to admit to the presence of cyborgs aboard." Cordelia leveled her stern gaze on everyone. Even Billie was a little intimidated by that look. "A hasty meeting was arranged, and we have tried to make lemonade out of lemons, as the expression goes. Chiron met with Amelia Aziner and a delegation from the colony. Long story short, the colonists, at first, demanded cyborg compliance. They wanted us to leave some of the men here. They wanted to bargain with me to trade for them, like commodities."

The disgust was clear in Cordelia's voice. Billie realized she—and a lot of the others—had come a long way in their beliefs about the man-machines who had saved them.

"We refused, of course," Roxy put in. "And then, Chiron had a few things to say to Mrs. Aziner."

Roxy looked smug, winking at her big cyborg as he smiled gently back. It was so clear to anybody watching them that they were in love. They were totally devoted to each other.

"They thought they could command the cyborgs to work in their factories, or in some other industry, until such time as another raid happened and they needed protection. Then, they just assumed the cyborgs would fight for them, without question."

"While we do, generally, like to help people out when we can," Medeus put in from his position standing beside Chiron, "we have no ties to this colony. We've only just become self-aware, again. None of us are willing to go back to being pawns. We're men with free will, and we won't work with anyone who doesn't understand that and respect it."

A chorus of agreeable murmurs rose from among the women.

"That's your right," Billie found herself saying. She hadn't meant to speak aloud, but when eyes turned to her, she elaborated, appealing to those sitting near her who looked undecided about all of this. "They didn't have to take us with them," she reminded her fellow refugees. "They could've left the station, and us, behind and never looked back. We owe them. At the very least, we owe them the respect due any other fellow human being."

Many of the doubters nodded at her words, and Billie couldn't help but look over to see Medeus's expression. It was almost unreadable, but there was something shining in his eyes. Something warm that made her feel as if he approved of her outburst.

"Well said," Cordelia complimented Billie. "There's more. Once Aziner realized she couldn't just command cyborg protection or trade for them, we really started talking. I think the biggest problem was that they saw us as either a threat or liars for not disclosing the presence of cyborgs aboard. Chiron was able to explain things."

"The gist of it is that we might be able to leave them with some protection when we go," Chiron said.

"The rail gun?" one of the ladies who'd been working with Roxy in the engine room asked.

Medeus nodded. "We're going to give it to them. We're not trading for it, exactly, though we're talking about accepting some parts that they can easily spare from which we hope to build a replacement for our own use. We'll advise them on where to install it for optimum coverage and provide detailed instructions for their people to get it down to the planet and mounted in place."

"Why don't a few of you just go downside to install it?" one of the women asked.

"A couple of reasons," Chiron replied. "First, none of us want to take the chance of not being allowed to return to the ship. We're safer up here where we have control of the systems. It's not likely, but the colonists could attempt imprisoning us, and then, we'd have to break out and cause damage. Maybe kill people in the process. We want to leave here as friends, not make more enemies."

"Secondly," Medeus picked up right where Chiron left off,

"we want the ship away from here before the weapon goes active. Just in case."

Some of the women looked frightened, but many nodded, understanding the cyborgs' reasoning. Billie knew there were probably a few more reasons that the men were keeping to themselves, but the first two were persuasive enough.

"Giving them the final pieces of the weapon will be the last thing we do before we undock," Medeus went on. "If all goes well, we're also willing to take a closer look around the system before we leave it entirely and see if we can find any clue as to where these raiders are, or have gone. Something's been interfering with trade to the colony, and it might be something simple that we can fix on our way out. I'd rather leave this place as friends. We might have to come back here someday for more supplies, and it's good to have at least one friendly port available during the storm in which we find ourselves."

Amelia seemed more than satisfied when she saw the first pieces of the rail gun being offloaded from the *Toby*. A few of the less-modified cyborgs were openly working in the cargo area now, observing and being observed by the people in the corridor of the station. It was all very tentative trust on the station folks' side, but also a subtle show of force from the cyborgs and refugees aboard the *Toby*.

Medeus had no doubt that the two defectors and their children had already told the station folk all they knew about the *Toby* and her crew. He felt betrayed a bit by those women and their kids but tried not to let it get him down. The support from the rest of the ladies meant a lot and was helping to boost morale among the cyborg crew. That was a good thing.

Perhaps the two who had abandoned ship had inadvertently caused a unification to occur that might otherwise have taken a lot longer. Maybe it would all work out for the best in the long run. He certainly hoped so.

That the majority of the women had spoken positively

about the cyborg influence on the ship was a good, visible improvement. The early days on the *Toby* had been filled with sidelong glances and mistrustful looks sent in the direction of the cyborg men by the female refugees. When nothing untoward had happened, and they all started working together a little more, things had gradually changed.

The women had lost some of the fear. They'd been more at ease around the men. But full acceptance hadn't yet arrived. Not for most of the men. Not for Medeus.

Chiron had his Roxy, and she was making great inroads in introducing him around to the rest of the ladies. They had been asking him all sorts of questions, and Medeus thought there was no better ambassador than the man who had awakened before all of them, and had successfully transitioned from cyborg to lover. Roxy helped, too. Her steadfast position beside Chiron and the rather obvious glow of happiness around her was very effective in disarming those who still felt a bit of mistrust in their hearts.

Medeus had it a little rougher than the others because of the obviousness of his repairs. He just *looked* more like a machine than most of the others. One of his eyes, half his face, most of his limbs, and more had been replaced with cybertronic parts. Unlike the other men, little time had been wasted on making his replacement parts look more like the original.

He had some truly gruesome-looking scars that the others didn't have. As if the doctors hadn't cared how he'd look after he was repaired. But they'd hidden the other cyborgs' scars, so why not his? He would never know, and hadn't really cared, until the refugees from *Eagle Nest Station* made him realize how scary he probably appeared to them.

He had never minded it...until now. When some of the children aboard stared, their eyes wide with fear as he passed, it bothered him. When the women moved to the other side of a passageway to give him a wide berth, he noticed, and it hurt.

But little things were helping him feel not quite so estranged. Billie's smile. Billie's admiring looks that she probably thought he hadn't noticed. Billie's kiss…

That kiss had rocked his world.

And the fact that she'd spoken out at that last meeting. She'd voiced her support in a way that had warmed the cold recesses of his mechanical heart. He hadn't really expected her to say anything, but when she did, he could hear the truth of her belief—her faith in his humanity. It had been a humbling moment.

A moment that gave him hope. Though he probably shouldn't even dream of such things. Chiron wasn't half as scary looking as Medeus. Just because Chiron had been able to commit to a woman and have her return the favor, didn't mean that Billie would succumb to Medeus's dubious charms.

Medeus watched the offload of the rail gun components from a position of concealment within the cargo hold. He did not want any of the station people to see him. The cyborgs had discussed it among themselves and decided that only those who looked mostly human should be seen by the colonists. It was all part of the plan to try to convince the colonists that they were, indeed, men. Not machines.

Medeus had pointed out to his fellows that their future was uncertain. It would be better to leave this colony as friends, rather than enemies. They might want to come back someday, so anything they could do now to smooth the way later, was a good thing.

He was surprised when Billie walked up to stand beside him. She stood in the hatchway behind which he monitored the offload via a combination of the cyborg network, visual relays, and floater cams in the hold. He stood carefully out of sight, but Billie was probably visible to anyone who looked closely.

"How's it going, Captain?" she asked, taking a look out the hatch herself.

"They should be finished shortly," he replied.

"I've got the course we discussed plotted and laid in," she said brightly. "Nav is ready when you are."

"Good to know," he said, wondering why she'd really

come down here.

Maybe it was just curiosity. Maybe she was nervous about getting free of the station. Or maybe... Dare he hope? Maybe she had just wanted to talk with him. Be around him in a less formal atmosphere than the bridge.

"I'm glad you stopped," he told her. "I wanted to thank you for speaking up at the meeting last night. That was kind of you."

She gave him a surprised look. "It was nothing less than the truth."

"Still..." His gaze met hers, and he noted that she didn't flinch. She had never flinched from looking at his ruined face. She was a very special woman, indeed. "You didn't have to say anything. I am grateful for your support."

She stepped closer to him, turning slightly to face him. "I..." She took a breath before continuing in a softer tone of voice. "I believe in you, Medeus. I know you and your brethren have probably all been through hell of one kind or another. I don't want any of us to cause any of you any more pain."

"That's..." He was so touched he had to stop and think for a moment how to reply.

But he wasn't to get the chance. One of the cyborgs within the cargo hold signaled at that moment. Amelia Aziner was standing at the dock entrance, where she could clearly see Billie—a face she recognized from previous encounters.

"Mrs. Aziner has some questions, Navigator," Jason relayed as he approached Billie. She turned away, and the moment was lost.

No matter. Medeus needed time to digest what she had said and the subtle nuances of her expression. They would be underway, soon, if all went as planned. He'd have time to talk to her, again, once he figured out what to say.

"Sorry. I'll handle her. Could you page Cordelia, just in case?" Billie asked him before turning to go.

He agreed as she walked through into the cargo hold and then to the wide dockside hatch through which cargo was loaded and unloaded. Medeus followed her progress with a floating cam, even as he sent an alert through the ship, requesting Cordelia's presence at dockside. Billie had left his side, but the fresh apple scent of her hair lingered in his brain.

CHAPTER 5

Billie sat at her nav station, preparing for departure. She was ready to get back out into space. She, like her father and older brother before her, felt most at home on the bridge, heading out on a course she had plotted. She'd often heard them describe the sensation, but until she had scraped up enough money to attend the space academy, she had never dreamed she would experience it, too.

Medeus walked onto the bridge, taking his place in the command chair, and all was right with her universe. At least for that moment. He was flipping switches, receiving reports from all stations around the ship, and generally making sure they were fit and ready to travel. He let Chiron handle the communications with the orbital station.

The people there had seen Chiron and had somehow come under the impression that he was the captain of the ship. Medeus didn't seem to mind. Billie supposed that had something to do with the damage done to his face. The surgeons had left Medeus looking a bit rougher than the other men. His face, in particular, showed the repair work. It was as if they'd done it on purpose. As if someone hadn't let the surgeons finish their job—either as punishment to Medeus or a warning to those who saw him.

Billie had a vivid imagination. She could easily believe that certain military elites hadn't wanted there to be any confusion between the former fleet commander and the cyborg that he had become. She had no doubt that the fleet commander's face had been very familiar to a vast number of military personnel. When he'd been blown up and rebuilt, there had to be some way to prevent confusion.

It was ghoulish, though, in her opinion. Cruel. Perhaps he'd had enemies, and those officers had wanted to destroy him visibly. If that was the case, they'd done a good job of it. But what made others afraid of him, only endeared him to Billie. It seemed so much harder for him than some of the others. His physical appearance was a barrier all by itself. It made people shy away from him. Billie had seen that from the first and vowed she would never do that to him. Never.

He was a man. With feelings. She truly believed that. No man who didn't feel could have kissed her the way he had. If only he would kiss her, again…and more. It was the stuff of her late-night fantasies, making love with Medeus. Something she seriously doubted he would ever let happen. Much to her disappointment.

"What did Mrs. Aziner have to say, Billie?" Medeus asked from right beside her. He'd snuck up on her, again, while she'd been contemplating naughtiness. She hoped he couldn't see the slight flush she knew was on her cheeks.

"She just wanted to verify some of the installation instructions. Jason helped with that. And then, she wanted to say how pleased she was with the gift of the rail gun and that we were welcome to return to the colony anytime." Billie thought over the long conversation she'd had with the old lady who ran the colony. "She also wanted to remind us about checking the system to see if we could figure out why no trade ships have been visiting. I said I'd remind the captain, which I am doing, right now." She smiled up at him, and he just shook his head, a slight grin playing around one corner of his mouth. She loved it when he smiled, even just that little bit.

"Thanks," he replied, losing some of the formality of his usual responses. She liked that even better.

When they were traveling on the in-system drive, heading for the delta quadrant of the system, Medeus kept his eye on target and tried not to think about his luscious navigator. Her work to this point had been superb. One of the men still checked her calculations, but that took mere moments, and they were all coming to trust her abilities more with each successfully charted course. She sat the nav boards alone now, with no cyborg watchdog.

When Medeus had told her she'd be nav first from now on, she had beamed. She'd smiled so hard he'd thought she might jump into his arms and hug him. Not that he'd have minded, but he had to discourage her from such things. He couldn't get any closer to her than he already was. He—for sure—couldn't kiss her, again. Not with his past standing between them.

"Captain, there's a buoy broadcasting a signal out-system," the man on the comms board said aloud. He was already receiving more detailed information from his fellow cyborg over their shared communications channel, but Medeus had requested that everyone on the bridge speak aloud, when there was time, for Billie's sake.

"Nav, can you put us in front of the signal? We need to hear what it's broadcasting." Medeus half-suspected this buoy, which was located on what would be the main trade route for most cargo ships, had been placed there by the raiders. The *Tobias Bay's* non-standard insertion into the system had made them miss the buoys altogether.

"Aye, sir. I've got a course," Billie replied, busily inputting numbers into the nav board.

Silently, Medeus reviewed the course she had plotted and found the path she had chosen to be both elegant and conservative of their resources—as had every course she had plotted so far. He flicked a silent message to Ajax, who had been tasked to check Billie's course computations because he'd been a pilot and captain of a small ship before his cyborganization. He'd had some nav training, as well, though he was not a specialist. He was acting as pilot, right now, and would implement any courses Billie plotted at the helm station.

Ajax ran the calculations and affirmed that Billie was on target, once again. Aloud, he said, "Course confirmed, Captain," giving Billie a gentle nod when she looked over at him.

Medeus could see her answering smile and almost wished it had been aimed at him, not his brother cyborg. But that way lay dangerous territory. He shook his head and concentrated on the matter at hand.

"Change course, helm," Medeus gave the order formally. "Let's see what that buoy is saying. Comms, play the message once you have it."

"Aye, Captain," Jason, the cyborg at the comms board, replied dutifully.

It took them about twenty minutes to put the ship at an angle where they could intercept the message. When he finally heard the whole thing, Medeus's suspicions were confirmed. The raiders had placed a false quarantine message, interdicting the colony and the entire system. Dire threats were made against any ship that dared cross the quarantine.

Such things had been done regularly throughout human space for as long as men had traveled the stars in ships. Some places were just too dangerous. Some solar systems were quarantined as navigation hazards when they contained unstable space-time. Some received no-fly-zone status due to hostile aliens or primitive cultures that needed to be protected.

Some—the scariest of the lot—were quarantined because of pathogens. Deadly plagues that could wipe out every last human being in the galaxy, should they get loose. That's the kind of warning that was on this buoy. It warned of a deadly plague that had run rampant through the colony, turning everyone there into disease-ridden monsters.

The message used all the right language. It sounded legal enough, but it clearly wasn't anything put in place by the central government. For one thing, the buoy was a commercially available model. The ones the government issued were much more high-tech. This model could be easily tampered with. In fact, that was Medeus's plan—to change the message and reverse the quarantine, warning anyone who heard the message that there had been raider activity in the system and to beware of strange ships.

"Comms," Medeus spoke to Jason, the cyborg who was best at doing such things, "change the message as we discussed and send a ping back to the colony with a recording of the original message, and our compliments. Tell them what we're doing to the buoy and lock that device down so nobody else can tamper with it the way we're going to."

"Aye, Captain." Jason smiled as he turned back to his station. *"This is gonna be fun,"* he commented along their private channel.

"Nav, what are the most common routes for vessels approaching the colony?" Medeus asked. "Put up a chart on the forward screen when you have it." Medeus knew it would take a few minutes for Jason to reprogram everything and lock it down.

Billie had the chart ready long before Jason was done, as Medeus had expected. She flashed it to the display, and Medeus studied it, along with everyone else on the bridge, except Jason, of course. He was clearly enjoying himself, if the nearly maniacal grin on his face was anything to go by. Medeus couldn't wait to hear the message Jason was crafting to put on the buoy.

"Good work," Medeus complimented Billie, even as he studied the paths other ships would take to get to Aziner Colony. "The most likely places for further buoys, based on the position of this one, are here and here." Medeus highlighted two areas on the chart with a simple command from his internal computer to the ship's system. "Nav, plot courses to intercept both points. I want to see if the raiders posted more quarantine notices and, if so, remove them."

"Aye, sir," Billie replied, already looking up numbers in her references.

They spent the rest of the day trolling around the system, intercepting message buoys and reprogramming them. Each time, they sent a message back to the colony, though from this far out, the colonists probably wouldn't receive the signals for a day or two. By the end of their search pattern, they had uncovered three more buoys, but that was it. Medeus was confident there were no more, and all four had been reprogrammed, and their code vandalized—in a good way—by Jason, enough that the raiders would never be able to use them as they had, again.

Jason had crafted a message that stated the colony has been under attack by slavers and to be on the lookout for pirates. They sent a copy of Jason's new buoy message back to the colony, along with the location of each of the buoys and command codes so they could control them remotely. The colonists might not have a ship capable of traveling to the buoys, but their signal would reach them, given time, and they could check periodically to make sure the buoys were still there. If one or more went missing, it would be a good indication that the raiders were back in the system, and the colonists might have time to prepare. Jason had rigged each of the buoys to report any traffic that passed within range back to the colony, which was as good an early-warning system as they could rig on short notice, and with no parts.

It was a small victory, but Medeus would take it. With any luck, the colonists would get some help, or at least some visits from trade ships. Perhaps they'd be able to prosper, once more. Or maybe, those who wanted to leave and head back for Earth would find passage.

A few colonists had inquired about leaving on the *Toby*, but once they realized rogue cyborgs were in charge and they had no plans to go anywhere near Earth or other places with a military presence, they soon stopped asking. It was just as well, Medeus thought. They had enough to deal with already. The women and children from *Eagle Nest Station* were really starting to come together to make the ship run smoothly.

The new hydroponics section was looking better and better each time Medeus went down there. He was pleased to see how many of the older kids were taking an interest and how many of the women had good prior experience in aquaculture. He was sure that, in time, they'd be producing their own vegetables, fruits, herbs, and even grains.

When Medeus finally went off shift, along with all the main-shift bridge crew, he headed for the hydroponics section. He wanted to see how it was going, and there shouldn't be any people there at this time of the cycle because it was main-shift dinner—a meal at which everyone would appear. For those on the later shifts, main-shift dinner served as either breakfast or lunch, but regardless of what sleep cycle people were on, it was good to gather as a whole group at least once per day.

He walked among the newly planted rows, enjoying the soft glow of the lighting as it mimicked sunset. The colonists had included a few starter seedlings that were already about halfway to maturation. They were in one section nearest the hatch. Medeus would start and end his informal tour there, among the immature greenery. The sprouts and small plants that symbolized hope for the future.

As he walked along, stretching his legs, he breathed in the fresh scent of sterilized dirt and water. The nutrient mixes and fertilizing compounds had different smells, depending on which crop was planted in them. The seedling trays were crowded with seeds that would be thinned and potted on once they sprouted, and each would sprout at different times, depending on the seed.

Medeus read the markers the gardeners had left clearly visible on each planted tray. Everything looked in order. They were making a good start of a system that would help feed them all.

Suddenly, the scent of apples came to him as if from a distance. Was he losing his mind? Was he imagining the scent of the woman he craved with every fiber of his being, even when she was nowhere near? Medeus looked around. He hadn't heard the hatch open, but there it stood…fifty feet away…open. With Billie leaning in and looking around. Had she come looking for him?

He got his answer when she spotted him, smiled then walked into the hold, letting the hatch close behind her. She walked on a direct path to his location. He stood perfectly still, not sure what to make of her appearance here, at this hour.

"You weren't at dinner," she began, as she stopped a few feet away from him. "Someone said they thought you had been coming down here when nobody was looking."

"I guess I haven't been as stealthy as I thought," he admitted, shaking his head slightly. "I wanted to check on progress. Growing our own food is a key step to making us more self-sufficient. We may not run into such understanding people as those of Aziner Colony in the future." He decided to add a bit more truth to his words. "And I like to see green, growing things. My father was a farmer, back on Earth. I grew up in Iowa. My first starship was a tractor. At least, I used to pretend the controls on the auto-tractor were starship controls when I snuck into the cab for a ride. The cab was my pretend command chair."

Her smile widened. "I used to play with the auto-nav on my mother's car, pretending I was plotting a course for hopping between solar systems."

She moved a step closer, the length of one of the 'ponics stations between them. He was at one end of the six-foot by three-foot unit, and she was at the other. They were, at least, both on the same side, along the same aisle, surrounded by similar units with only enough room to push a collection cart between them.

The lights kept dimming at a very slow, steady pace, in

pretend-sunset. The atmosphere was intimate, even though they were in a huge cargo hold. The rows of lights just a few feet over the growing beds and the units themselves created a sense of the big space being crowded, even if it wasn't really true.

"I guess we weren't so different as kids," he said, taking a step closer to her, even though he knew it wasn't wise. His head wasn't in control, right now. No, other things...farther down his body...were guiding his motions at this moment.

"I guess not," she agreed, moving another step closer until there was only about two feet separating them, near the center of the 'ponics unit. "So...why didn't you come to dinner? Aren't you hungry?"

"I'll get something later," he said offhandedly. "I needed some quiet time to think about...things. And I don't like to come here when the kids are working. They..."

"They're scared of your appearance," she said, not unkindly. "Which really is all the more reason that you *should* come down here and show them that you're not really scary at all."

He had to chuckle at her boldness. "I'm not scary? Really?" He moved involuntarily closer. "Billie, I have looked in the mirror."

"Then, your mirror must be broken, because the man I see when I look at you is a good man. A kind man. A powerful man." She moved right up against him, and with his one hand on the rim of the 'ponics unit, it felt natural to put his other arm around her waist. "When I look at you, I see a man who is scarred, but stronger for it," she told him.

"You really see me that way?" he asked. He had to hear it again. "As a man?"

"As a man I'm very attracted to, Medeus. A man I'd like to get to know a lot better." She moved, and then, they were kissing.

This was nothing like that first tentative kiss on the bridge. This was an all-out flame-throwing, hold-onto-your-britches kiss. He went from zero to light speed in no time flat, and he knew… He knew… This time, he wouldn't be able to let her go. This time, he wouldn't be able to be noble.

But, then… Nobility—sometimes—was over-rated.

CHAPTER 6

Billie couldn't believe she had done it. She'd made the move on Medeus she'd been thinking about ever since that first kiss. She'd tracked him down when she'd become concerned by his absence at dinner. Sam was busy with his friends, staying over at one of the other cabins tonight, so she was free to do as she wished. And lately, all her wishes had revolved around Medeus…and his kiss. When she'd found him alone, she'd pounced. Well, maybe not *pounced*, but she'd moved closer and closer, and then, somehow, she'd found the courage to take a chance.

She was so glad, at this moment, that she'd done it. His kiss was all she'd ever wanted. His passion was incendiary. This was no polite joining of lips, soon to part. No, this was a claiming. A torrid inferno of desire that wanted what it wanted and wouldn't quit until it got it. Glory, hallelujah!

The cargo hold was deserted, except for a few thousand plants. It was just the two of them, in an ever-dimming room. The sunset cycle had started a while back, and the pale yellow glow of the artificial lights had been programmed to give the seeds and plants the right growing conditions. What it gave the two people standing among the plant beds was an intimacy that was both unexpected and welcome.

In essence, night was falling...as if they were on a planet somewhere. It was romantic, in its way. And the increasing darkness also increased the intimacy of the moment.

When Medeus lifted her off her feet, his hands supporting her rump, she felt a pang of desire rise through her body. Where was he taking her? It didn't really matter. He just had to keep holding her, kissing her, walking slowly, but with purpose...somewhere.

The answer came a few moments later when he placed her on one of the tables that had been set up adjacent to the plant area. It was just the right height, and the hold beyond the table was completely dark, now. Only a faint glow came from the lights over the growing beds. There were marker beacons around the edges of the hold that would stay on at all times to illuminate the hatches, but other than that, they were in a world of their own.

She opened her legs, and he stepped between as he kissed her, again and again. It was just about perfect... Except for all the fabric keeping their bodies apart. That had to go.

She pushed at his uniform. The cyborgs wore a mix of civilian clothing they'd found aboard the ship and their old uniforms, but Medeus always turned up for duty in his battle togs. She thought they were sexy, but just at the moment, they were in the way.

He didn't seem to want to help her get to his skin, but he apparently had no compunction against ridding her of her clothing. Her top came off over her head with his help. Her bra didn't last long, either. And then, she felt his fingers tracing the curves of her breasts, cupping, squeezing gently and touching in ways that made her gasp with pleasure.

He lifted her off the countertop briefly to remove her pants. She'd kicked off her shoes, so there was nothing to stop her pants from sliding right off over her feet and to the deck. She was naked, her cyborg between her spread thighs. He was still fully clothed, but she wouldn't push him. She thought she understood his hesitancy to show her what had been done to his body, and that sparked her compassion. They had time...she hoped. She would teach him that she didn't mind his scars—except for how they affected him.

For now, she just needed him to disrobe in certain areas so they could get on with the pleasure and put away the doubt. She pushed at his hips, fingering the waistband of his combat trousers with demanding motions. He kissed her and, at the same time, unfastened the waistband and lowered the closure that would allow his hard cock to spring free.

She was pleased to see that at least that part of him looked like original equipment. She smiled as she reached between them to touch his hardness. She wouldn't make him wait long, but she wanted just a moment to savor this. She scooted forward on the countertop until she was in position for maximum penetration. She didn't want to take this slow. No, she wanted it all. Hard and fast, and...breathtaking.

"Now, please," she begged him, unable to form full sentences. He seemed to understand what she meant, anyway.

Taking only a moment to check her readiness—moment that made her squirm with want and nearly cry out with need—he removed his fingers and came into her slowly.

It wasn't the hard, fast claiming she'd envisioned, but it was so much better. Hard, slow, deliberate. He watched the place where they joined and then looked up into her eyes, holding her gaze as he slid all the way home. Then, he waited. His gaze bore into hers as his body joined with hers for these delicious minutes.

"More," she whispered, when the tension got to be too great. Billie saw, in his eyes, the split second that he gave into the need and began to move.

First slow, then faster with each delectable thrust, he came into her, again and again. She took all he would give and wanted more. So much more. She wanted all of him, but she'd take whatever he was willing to give, and be happy. If she could somehow get him to the point where he would trust her with the rest of his rebuilt body, she would count that a victory, but this was enough for now.

He pushed into her, over and over, driving her passion higher. She clung to him, her fingers digging into his shoulders. Strong shoulders that seemed to bear so much with such dignity.

She admired everything about him—the imperfections along with the strength of his personality and will. He was a good man, straight down to his core.

Her crisis came, and she shook with pleasure as he held her through it. He brought her to an even higher peak, in time, and when she could take no more, he joined her in climax, holding her close as their bodies strained together.

Medeus held Billie tight to his chest, never wanting the moment to end. The moment he'd rediscovered his manhood. His humanity…on the most basic level. She had given him this gift, and he would value her forever for it.

He still had a fear of hurting her, but being with her had become an imperative. Something he could no longer live without. He wanted her by his side at all times and he wanted to secure her affection in any way possible. It was both shocking and scary, but he could no longer deny what was within his rusty heart.

"Come back to my cabin," she murmured, stroking her lips along his jaw, long moments later. "Sam's sleeping at a friend's tonight, so I've got the place to myself. I don't want this to end, yet."

He couldn't lie to her. Not now. Not ever. "I don't either," he told her.

He stepped away, found her clothing and helped her put them back on. He liked her naked, but it would be risky to run down the corridor of the ship—even while everyone else was supposedly at dinner.

Dressed again, they walked, hand in hand, down the empty passageway to her cabin, which, thankfully, wasn't far. He wasn't sure how he would have reacted if anyone had seen them. He wasn't concerned about cyborgs. They all knew something was up because he'd been out of touch for longer than allowable and had been answering inquiries over the silent comm with requests for privacy.

Chiron had intervened when others had worried, and Medeus had told Chiron the truth of what was happening and why he wanted privacy. Chiron had then gone on to tell the others to leave Medeus alone and not to worry. He wasn't seeking privacy to do something drastic. Rather, he was getting lucky.

Such a juvenile term for what felt like a universe-altering event. When they got to her cabin, Medeus followed her to the bed. It wasn't huge, but it would hold them both comfortably. He didn't want to be a cad, though, so he simply sat with her for a bit. He wanted to talk with her—almost as much as he wanted to make love with her again. He craved the closeness of sharing thoughts and feelings that he hadn't experienced with a woman in far too long.

All his fellow cyborgs were men. Military men. He had held one of the highest ranks among them, and there was a definite divide—even now—between the high-ranking officers and the others. He had tried to open up with Chiron and had been somewhat successful, but Medeus sensed he could say things to Billie that he couldn't say to the others.

Whether she would hate him afterwards... Well, that remained to be seen.

There was still the giant stumbling block of her older brother between them, though she didn't know it. He would save that for... Well...maybe never. He wasn't sure if he could deal with the emotional fallout that was sure to come if he revealed his involvement in Alex's demise.

Still, the longer she was on the bridge with him and the more he remembered his human existence, the more she reminded him of that other Latimer navigator he'd known. Quick witted and bright eyed. A natural nav—something that didn't come along often and was to be admired and respected. Medeus had held Alex Latimer in high esteem. He felt the same about Alex's sister's skills on the nav station and was privileged to watch them come into their full power.

But, on a more personal note, he just liked *her*. She was efficient, smart and beautiful in every way. The more he got to know her, the more he loved her.

Damn. *Love*. That slowed his racing thoughts right down.

"I love what they did with the new 'ponics section," Billie said as she moved about her sleep chamber, clearing space for him—or so it seemed. "It's going to be amazing when everything starts to really grow."

"I always liked walking among the growth beds on my ships," he admitted, "from the time I was just out of the academy until…" He trailed off. He hadn't meant to bring up his last command, but he wasn't thinking clearly. That notion of being in *love* with Billie had sort of shorted out his brain a little.

"Until your last ship, right? It was some kind of heavy cruiser?" she asked, innocently enough. She had no idea the verbal minefield he had to walk through to talk about the *Vanguard*—especially with her.

The military didn't generally supply the nitty-gritty details of a loved one's death to the family, but the *Vanguard's* destruction had been enough of a sensation that the story had leaked out. The ship had taken enemy fire, but what really killed it was a methane leak.

Medeus had looked it up in the classified databases after he started to awaken. A few survivors in forward compartments told the tale. Debris had ruptured one of the oxygen lines and when leaking methane from the recycling system hit that, it blew the ship apart from within. The military had changed the design of that entire class of ships since the *Vanguard's* demise because they finally realized the recycling systems were just too close to the oxygen tanks. Medeus lamented privately that it had only taken a thousand deaths to help them figure it out.

"It was a cruiser," he told her. "The destruction of it took me by surprise, which it shouldn't have. We were in battle and a lucky shot by the enemy in just the wrong spot caused irreparable damage that ultimately killed the ship and most of my crew." He tried hard not to sound devastated but knew some of it leaked out, anyway.

She sat down next to him and put a hand on his shoulder. He looked at her and caught the compassion in her gaze. It was like a lifeline being tossed to a man lost at sea.

"I'm sorry," she said, the simple words touching him deeply.

He moved closer, taking her free hand in his and raising it to his lips for a gentle kiss. "You're too good to me."

"You still blame yourself for the destruction of your ship, regardless of the fact that it was caused by battle damage?" She shook her head slowly. "You weren't to blame. You did the best you could at the time. If you want someone to blame…blame the enemy." She moved her hand from his shoulder to his cheek. "You were not at fault."

He couldn't make her understand without revealing too much. He didn't want this time with her to end, though he knew it probably would in the not-too-distant future. He couldn't keep lying to her by omission. Not when she was so understanding and kind-hearted. He couldn't give her less than the truth… Even if the truth would drive her away from him.

But not just yet.

"You're too forgiving," he said quietly, and hoped she'd let the matter drop. "I just wish…"

"What?" she asked.

"Sometimes, I wish I had my old life back. That I was in command of something with a real chance to help send the jit'suku back where they came from," he told her. "Part of me wants to go back and help fight the war, but I know I can't."

"Even after all you've been through, you still want to help fight the invasion?" she asked, seeming surprised.

"I'm still human. Or, rather, I was," he said. "I'm not sure what I am, now, but the human part of me is still there."

She tucked herself into his arms. "Of course it is," she said with quiet belief in her tone. "You're as human as I am, but you've been through hell and back to reclaim your identity."

She got it. She really did. How had he ever been so blessed to find a woman who understood him, perhaps better than he understood himself?

They spent the rest of the night in Billie's cabin, making love, talking and just generally getting to know each other. He kept his undershirt on, but she'd convinced him to take off his pants completely. She wasn't afraid of his scars, but she also didn't want to push him too hard. He'd already come a long way.

It was a special night that she enjoyed with every fiber of her being. And, when her alarm went off to signal the start of a new day aboard the *Toby*, Medeus was gone.

It still made no sense to her how a man that huge could move so silently. He'd left without waking her, but she knew he'd been there from the mussed sheets, and the single stalk of lavender he must have taken from the seedlings in the 'ponics section and placed in a cup of water on her bedside table.

Evidence that he'd left and come back. And *still*, she hadn't heard a sound. She shook her head as she breathed in the delicate scent of the rare bloom. There had only been a few lavender flowers, and they'd been in a protected part of the beds, to keep folks from taking them. Of course, nobody denied the captain when he wanted something, but she doubted he had actually asked anyone. He'd just used his cyborg-ninja skills to go into the cargo hold and spirit this bloom away.

She loved that he'd done that for her. A simple gesture that meant a lot to her. She might even start believing that he…cared.

Billie didn't have time to ponder it too long because she had to get ready for her day. She wanted to check on Sam before he went to the big cabin they'd set aside to be the schoolroom. She had been so busy since they came aboard that she hadn't spent a lot of time with her little brother, but by the looks of things, he was coping much better with their drastic change in circumstances than she was.

Sam hadn't had a lot of friends his age on the station, but at least a few of those children had come aboard the *Toby* with their mothers, so he had a few familiar faces in his class as well as some new kids he hadn't met before. He was at the age where he wasn't quite so dependent on her anymore and was starting to stretch his wings. She was glad because she'd just been too involved with the ship and learning her trade as a navigator. She felt bad about it, but Sam didn't seem to notice. He was happy here, on the ship, where he seemed to think every day was a new adventure.

She stopped in to see him before classes started and gave him a quick hug, though he had started shying away from displays of emotion a few months ago. She couldn't help herself. Sam was the only family she had in the universe and she loved him, even if he was starting to show his independence. She left him with the teachers and went to the bridge, lighter of heart for seeing him. She had a full shift today, though she wasn't quite sure how she was going to get through it without drifting off to fantasyland every time she looked at Medeus. He'd transported her to another world entirely last night. Several times.

Her cheeks heated, just thinking about it. She hoped she could control her blushes on the bridge, or the very observant cyborg crew might notice.

As she was approaching the bridge, a thought made her pause. The cyborgs had some kind of near-instant comms. Did that mean they all knew what she'd done with Medeus last night?

Her jaw dropped, and her cheeks went from flushed to pale as she looked at her face reflected off the shiny comm panel on the corridor wall. *Damn.* They probably all knew already.

She straightened her shoulders and started walking again. Well. If they already knew, then she wouldn't have to worry about anybody figuring anything out on the bridge, where they were all cyborgs, anyway. No, she only had to worry about everywhere else on the ship where she might run into her fellow refugees. The women would gossip, as they had about Roxy and Chiron. Billie didn't think she'd mind for her own sake, and she didn't think anybody would hassle young Sam, but it might bother Medeus.

She didn't want anything to frighten him off. Not gossip. And certainly not his past. She'd remembered a few things last night that made her suspicious about who he had once been. She already planned to do a bit of subtle database searching when she went off shift later, but if what she thought she remembered was true, then there might be more between them than a bit of grapevine gossip.

When she arrived for her shift on the bridge, Medeus was professional and courteous. So much so that Billie almost wondered if she had dreamed the passionate lover of the night before. But then, she'd catch him looking at her in a certain way, and all the heat of the night before would come flooding back into her veins.

She had it bad if just a smoldering look from him could send her from zero to ready-for-action in no time flat. She didn't mind. Not really. Not now that she knew how good it could be between them. His gaze promised more, and she'd take all she could get, if he was willing to continue.

They'd been cruising around the system that was home to the Aziner Colony all day, looking for evidence of the raiders, but hadn't seen much until late in the shift. At that point, Ajax picked up some traces of gravitational disturbances of the kind often left behind by badly tuned jump drives.

Medeus asked Roxy to take a look at the data, and she confirmed what they had surmised. A large ship with badly tuned drives had been in the area recently. What's more, it gave them a way to trace its movements that Billie didn't quite understand. Regardless, she was happy to plot the course information Ajax relayed, to come up with a visual of where the badly tuned drive had been traveling through the system…and where it had left.

Other than that single trace, no other evidence was found of any other ships traversing the system. With the interdiction message on all the buoys, that wasn't surprising. Anyone who might've been on approach had been warned off from far enough out that they could just move along to their next destination without ever going closer to the colony. Whoever had left the traces hadn't been concerned about the quarantine, which strongly indicated that they might have been the ones who put the buoys out in the first place. It was a long shot, but it was at least something. A faint trail to follow.

The question then became... Should they pursue?

CHAPTER 7

After speaking with Cordelia to set up another ship-wide meeting that evening after dinner, Medeus left the bridge last—with Billie. She had fluttered around her workstation, *cleaning*, ostensibly, until the others had left. She'd wanted a chance to speak with Medeus, if he was so inclined.

While the second-shift cyborgs settled into their positions, Billie and Medeus met in the hallway, just outside the hatch, which closed behind them. When the bridge was manned, the guard was stationed inside. When at dock, the guard was in the corridor. Since they were underway, that meant an empty corridor, with just the two of them walking side by side.

They didn't speak until they reached the point where they would have to either split up or continue on together. Medeus paused.

"Can I meet you for dinner?" he asked suddenly, as if he had been saving up the question and was concerned she might say no.

That small insecurity touched her heart. "Of course," she told him.

Billie often ate at a table near or even with some of the

cyborgs she knew. She thought she had been doing her part to bridge the gap between the human refugees and the cyborg crew. A few of the women followed her example, some with children who were fascinated by the cyborgs—just like Sam. Some of the young boys saw the men as heroes out of their comic vids, she knew.

Billie doubted anyone would gossip about her having dinner with Medeus, except to say that it was odd he would join them at all. He usually wasn't one to participate in the communal meals. Of course, tonight, there would be a meeting. That would explain his presence readily enough.

"Good," he said, sounding a little relieved. "I have a bit more work to do before dinner, but I'll definitely see you there, all right?"

He stepped closer, and she did the same. "All right," she replied softly, hoping he was going to kiss her.

And then…he did. It was an all-too-brief kiss of parting, but it steadied her. He wasn't pulling away from her. The kiss was a statement of continued interest. He'd had to be businesslike for the past hours on the bridge, but she understood now. Just like her, underneath the surface, there had been that smoldering river of desire that had not stopped, but had merely been contained while they worked.

When he stepped back, she felt momentarily dizzy. He had that effect on her. He smiled gently, a look of such caring on his scarred face that she almost caught her breath.

"I'll see you at dinner, then," he reiterated, holding her shoulders indulgently while she caught her balance.

"Yeah," she replied, lost for words and sense until he stepped completely away and left down the side corridor.

Billie went the other way after standing there immobile for a few moments, just watching him walk away. He turned at the last moment and caught her eye, sending her a grin and a wink, if she wasn't very much mistaken. He *knew* the effect he had on her, and he seemed to be amused by it. The stinker.

Then again, she couldn't blame him. She was putty in his hands, and it was useless to try to hide it. Why would she?

She *liked* being with him. Everything about him tickled her fancy, and his mysteries only made him more attractive.

Which reminded her… She had some research of her own to do.

An hour and a half later, when Billie sat back from her screen, she sighed heavily. Sam didn't notice. He was sitting on the floor using the low table in front of the couch in the main room of their suite, doing his homework. Thankfully, Sam was a good student and enjoyed the challenge of school. He especially liked mathematics, which didn't surprise Billie. Everyone in their family was good at math. You had to be, if you wanted to be a navigator.

She was also pretty good at research, and her suspicions had been confirmed more easily than she'd expected. All she had to do was read Alex's last few letters and then do a little searching through news files that were archived on her personal tab. She'd put two and two together and had come up with a heartbreaking story.

Medeus was—or had been—a close friend of her brother's. His commander, but also a man he respected greatly and even called friend. Theirs had been an odd pairing. Most commanders didn't get too close with their bridge crew, because they moved around a lot, changing from ship to ship all the time, but Alex's special gift for nav had made him more valuable than most.

Commander Michael Bennet had specifically arranged to keep Alex with him from ship to ship, as he rose in rank. They'd traveled the stars together, as a team, for many years. Because of that, they'd become friends, of a sort.

Alex had talked about Captain Bennet, then Commander Bennet, then Fleet Commander Bennet in quite a few of his letters home. Occasionally, he referred to the man simply as *Michael*. There had been deep respect in Alex's words when he spoke of Michael Bennet, and after knowing Medeus, even for this short while, Billie understood why.

If Medeus had been Michael Bennet—and she was almost

certain that was the case—then he'd been, and still was, a man of deep character, who inspired others to do their best at all times. He set a prime example for his men, and he accepted no less than peak performance. She supposed it was a bit easier with a crew made up of cyborgs, but he'd applied the same standards aboard the *Toby* as he had aboard every ship he'd commanded… Until his untimely death aboard his flagship, the *Vanguard*.

The question was, now that she knew who he had been, how did that make her feel? She sat back, thinking about it for long time. She knew Alex had spoken of his deep admiration for Michael Bennet and had thought he was lucky to have had his career hitched to that of one of the fastest rising commanders in the human military. Bennet hadn't risen through the ranks due to nepotism or bribery. He'd gotten there because of his achievements. The honest way.

It was often said, if not for the fault in the design of the *Vanguard*, Bennet would have become one of the youngest admirals ever. Based on his record, Billie could easily believe that. It wasn't just something his colleagues had said to be kind at his funeral.

The fact that he had been commanding when Alex was killed… Well, that was just circumstances beyond anyone's control. Did she blame Medeus for her brother's death? No. She could state that quite emphatically. All the reports had talked about the design of the ship, in detail, once the investigations had been concluded.

She didn't believe there had been any sort of cover-up. There was no reason to lie about how the *Vanguard* had been destroyed. They could just as easily have blamed human error, hiding the problem with the design of the ship. But there had been survivors. Those survivors had demanded the truth, and the story was sensational enough in the media that they'd gotten it.

An exhaustive investigation had concluded that a series of unusual events had fatally exposed a serious design flaw in the new class of ships. The *Vanguard* had been the first completed—and the first destroyed. After that, all of those ships had gone back to the yards for an immediate refit, if they were already in use. Those that were still on the assembly lines had been retooled.

That, more than anything, calmed her. Her brother had died as a victim of circumstance. Nothing Medeus could have done would have changed the outcome. They'd all been doomed by the very design of the ship, itself. If anyone was to blame, it was whoever had cut corners and not foreseen the dire results of their design choices.

By the time the dinner chime sounded throughout the ship, Billie had made peace with the new information she had discovered. If only to help her know him better, she was glad she had learned the truth. Maybe, someday, Medeus would feel comfortable enough with her to speak of it, himself. She wouldn't push. His past was a sore subject, she knew. She probably shouldn't have snooped, but now that it was done, she was glad. Knowing what had come before gave her new insights into his behavior.

She put away her personal tab and tried to put the letters from Alex out of her mind. She was going to have dinner with her lover, and her dead brother's last words to her were better left in the past, where they belonged. She'd loved Alex, but she'd had to learn to let the grief over his passing go. She had a new life, now, as a navigator in her own right. It had been hard-won, but she loved her new job, even if the situation wasn't exactly ideal.

With a lighter heart, she herded Sam down the corridor to the dining hall. A crowd had already gathered. There would be a meeting after dinner, and everyone had shown up to see what was going on.

Billie and Sam took their places along the periphery of the room, in the area where the ladies ended and the cyborgs began. There was some mixing in the middle, but the crew was still far too segregated from the passengers, in Billie's opinion. She hoped that, in time, the two groups would meld more and form friendships, but they'd only been traveling together a relatively short period. She knew that real friendships took time to build.

Billie and Sam had already gone through the cafeteria line and filled their trays when Medeus arrived. He waved to her discreetly then picked up the tray for himself, moving along the line and selecting what he would eat for dinner. When he had his tray filled, he joined her at the table she'd claimed in the zone between the two groups.

"Mind if I join you?" Medeus asked. Billie saw her little brother's eyes just about pop out of his head. He'd asked her so many questions about the cyborgs and especially their captain that she'd finally forbidden the subject altogether.

"Not at all, Captain. Have you met my little brother, Sam?" She knew Sam wasn't scared. His expression told the story. He was thrilled.

"Pleased to make your acquaintance, Mister Latimer," Medeus replied with grave seriousness in his tone, though his eye sparkled with mischief.

"Nobody calls me that. I'm just Sam," her little brother insisted. "And you're the captain."

"That I am, just Sam," Medeus answered as he sat down and settled his tray before him. Sam cracked up at the little joke and Billie smiled at Medeus. He was such a good man, and he seemed to be good with Sam, which was a relief.

As they began eating, she noticed a few of the women nearby commenting on his appearance at dinner. Medeus didn't often mingle, so he was notable by his presence.

When Ajax and Jason came over to join them, Billie smiled and welcomed them, though inwardly she longed for a quiet candlelit dinner for two. She wasn't sure where she would find such a romantic setting aboard the *Toby*, but a girl could dream, couldn't she?

Sam was overjoyed at meeting more cyborgs, so she couldn't complain too much. When the captain introduced him as "just Sam" the little boy started laughing again and Billie noticed the effect Sam's laughter was having on everyone else. The women seemed intrigued and a lot less intimidated, which Billie figured was a step in the right direction.

Medeus didn't mind the silent ribbing he was taking from Ajax, Jason, and the rest of his cyborg brethren as he sat with Billie and her little brother for dinner. He took it as a sign of growing camaraderie between them all. Those who had fully embraced their returning emotions were amused at his delicate dance around their navigator. Those who were just starting to remember what it was like to feel were bemused and observant.

He didn't mind being a learning experience for them. They all had this difficult road to navigate of not only remembering who they'd been but trying to integrate those memories and feelings back into some kind of life. The fact that Chiron, and now, apparently, Medeus had found a way to attract one of the females on the *Toby* seemed to give the others heart.

Not that all the men were ready for such things. But, when they were, there was hope that they might find a female willing to love them. He liked being able to give the others a bit of hope…even if Medeus knew his romance with Billie had probably been doomed from the outset because of his past.

He kept that knowledge firmly to himself. There were some things his fellow cyborgs didn't need to know.

When dinner was over, a few of the women took the younger children off to play before the meeting started. Medeus took his place at the front of the large room without comment. He was always aware of Billie, regardless of where she was. He seemed to have a special sort of radar where she was concerned. He thought dinner with Billie and her little brother had gone well. Medeus had feared that Sam would be afraid of his scars, but the boy seemed more intrigued than frightened, so Medeus counted that as a win.

As he began speaking, outlining what they had learned, he knew Billie was watching him. He did his best not to look over at her, lest the women start gossiping. He would do all he could to protect her, even from something as ephemeral as gossip.

"We found traces of a ship entering and exiting the system," Medeus told the assembly. The cyborgs already knew everything, but he had to lay it out verbally for the women. "Since the message buoys seem to have effectively quarantined the system, this is suspicious, and there is a good chance the ship that was moving freely about the system belongs to the slavers who raided the Aziner Colony. What we need to discuss is what to do about it, if anything. Our ship is fully stocked. We have several choices to make about our future. Where to go next, for example. Considering the trail we found, do we pursue the raiders and try to learn more about where they came from or where they went? Or do we keep our noses out of it and head for some other destination?"

The discussion that followed was lively and, at times, contentious. Many of the women—especially those with children—pointed out the possible danger involved in going after raiders. Medeus called on several of his fellow cyborgs to explain how they might be able to follow the trail without actually exposing themselves to too much danger, though, of course, there was always the possibility of unforeseen events.

There was a strong desire among many in the room to at least investigate, as much as they could, where the slavers might have either come from or gone to, in order that they could then inform the colony or maybe tip off some authority—anonymously, of course. Medeus was glad to see there was a strong desire for justice among the female passengers. He, himself, favored further exploration and investigation, but the reality was, their ship was old and slow. It also had no weapons to speak of, even though two teams of men were working steadily on the creation of those rail guns.

At some point, they'd have to stop for a few hours to let a few of the cyborgs go out in pressure suits so they could mount their new weapons to the hull. Mounting the weapons would take finesse. Mechanically, it was pretty straight forward, but they didn't want the weapons to be obvious, until they were needed. Which meant hidden mounts in strategic places that could take the stresses of repeated firing, if necessary.

There had been several silent debates among the cyborg contingent already on how best to mount the guns, but they'd eventually come to a consensus, and plans were being made. They would take a few hours to put the guns in place while in the relative safety of this system, before they went off anywhere. Deciding where to go, though, would take time, so they needed to get that process started now.

They'd gathered all the intel they could from this system. Presenting it to the women of the *Toby* had been the next logical step. Getting them to talk about it and come to some sort of decision would take longer than the same process among cyborgs, due to their lack of a private comm. The cyborgs could share thoughts at the speed of the computer processors inside their brains. The women had to communicate their ideas the old fashioned way.

Medeus figured the time it took for the women to decide would probably coincide with the time it would take the men to mount the weapons. They had planned to do some limited testing to align the targeting on each of the rail guns. They had the completed original—the mate to the one they'd given the colonists—and the one they'd started making from the spare parts provided by the colonists was also nearing completion. They could begin the mounting process shortly.

First though, he had to get the women debating their next course of action. The cyborgs already had their consensus, but they had to respect the will of their passengers, as well. After a good hour of discussion, when they were going around in circles, Medeus decided to let the ladies think things over for a while before they brought the matter to a vote.

He left the dining hall, knowing the debate went on without him. The other cyborgs left, in small groups, until it was just the civilians left to discuss and debate among themselves. Medeus knew Billie would be in the thick of it, probably being pelted with questions since she was on the bridge and knew first-hand what they'd seen of the other ship's traces.

Chiron stayed behind, too. His place was with Roxy now, and he was the perfect conduit to keep the cyborgs in the loop about what the women discussed. He wasn't thrilled with the idea of being a spy, but he also didn't want to leave Roxy on her own. They were a couple now, in the first bloom of their relationship. They wanted to be together all the time.

Besides, it couldn't hurt for the women to see at least one of the cyborgs as a besotted fool who was deeply in love. Attitudes toward the rest of the guys had lightened considerably since Chiron and Roxy had gone public with their love affair. Chiron even planned to ask the Chief Engineer to marry him, as soon as he found the right moment. All the cyborgs knew, but had been sworn to secrecy. Nobody wanted to ruin the moment for Chiron…or for his lady.

Thinking of the happy couple made Medeus wonder about his own ill-fated romance with Billie. He loved her. He'd come to that devastating conclusion already. But how could he declare his feelings with so much standing between them? He was very much afraid he had doomed himself—and possibly Billie—to heartbreak. He cursed himself for every kind of fool. He shouldn't have allowed anything to start between them. Not with his past. Not with the burden on his shoulders of what his past had cost Billie and her little brother.

The more he thought about it, the more uncomfortable he became with lying to her, even by omission. The honorable thing, he knew, would be to break it off before she became any more involved emotionally. He was already lost. He loved her, and he'd admitted it to himself. It would be the height of cruelty on his part if he let her fall in love with him and then the truth came out.

He didn't want to hurt her like that. He didn't want to hurt her—ever. But that ship had already sailed. His former self had gotten Alex killed…or worse. He couldn't be certain the military hadn't turned more of his former crew into cyborgs.

The guilt he still felt over the loss of the *Vanguard* would stand between him and Billie forever, he realized in a moment of clarity. It wasn't something he could just continue to ignore. Not for long, anyway.

He would have to end it. That was the least cruel thing to do. She might be confused and a bit angry at first, but that was nothing compared to the way she would feel when she discovered the truth. This way, only he would be left brokenhearted.

Medeus knew what he had to do—now the only question was if he could find the courage to do it.

CHAPTER 8

The women took less time than the cyborgs expected to come to a consensus. Chiron reported from inside the dining hall that the women had nearly unanimously voted to try to follow the trail left by what they presumed to be the raiders' ship, at least a little farther. Leaving the innocents of Aziner Colony to suffer in fear of the next raid didn't sit well with the women of the *Tobias Bay*.

While they weren't willing to risk their own safety too much, they had decided the least they could do was follow the trail and see what they could discover from what they hoped would be a safe distance. Besides, they had reasoned, they really didn't have any other destinations in mind that would work for their cyborg saviors. The only places the women knew were well within human-controlled space, which meant a military presence, particularly in wartime.

A military presence that would, no doubt, try to make slaves of the cyborgs once more. The women wanted safety, but not at the expense of the men who had literally saved their lives. They had not forgotten the risk the cyborgs had taken to get every last person who wanted to go off *Eagle Nest*

Station.

Medeus felt warmth in his heart on hearing this. His trust had been abused a bit by the two women who had revealed their presence on Aziner Colony, but the rest had proven, once again, that not all humans were untrustworthy. In fact, most were upstanding individuals who had a sense of honor, even if they had never served in the military. Medeus respected them and their deliberation process. He couldn't run this ship like a military vessel where his word, as captain, was the law. No, he had to do things a lot more subtly here. He was glad the women were giving him no cause to regret his decision to do so.

That night, Billie waited in her bedroom after tucking Sam in, but Medeus didn't come to her. She went out looking for him at one point, but the cyborgs had closed ranks, and nobody would reveal where Medeus was hiding. Hiding. From her.

She was angry at first, then hurt. Then, she started to think about how he might be feeling. She knew he'd been confused from the moment his memories had started returning. What if he remembered Alex? What if being around Billie reminded him too much of the friend he had lost? What if he had some misguided macho thing about sleeping with a friend's sister?

She went back to her room and did her best to sleep. She would give him time to figure himself out, but she would corner him at some point, and then, she vowed, they would talk.

The next day shift on the bridge offered her little time for personal talk, but she did get a chance to learn some fascinating new ways to follow gravitational trails through space. Medeus encouraged her to tap into that sixth sense she and her family seemed to have about navigation, and when they transitioned back to regular space, following a path she had crafted from both data *and* instinct, she was gratified to find them on the edge of a populated system.

A populated system that didn't appear on any of the star

charts. Now, wasn't that interesting?

"Can they see us?" Billie whispered, but the cyborgs, with their superior senses, heard her, of course.

"Probably not this far out," Ajax answered, sitting the board beside hers. "Not unless they have some serious military-grade scan hardware, and even that is rare."

"And classified," Medeus reminded his fellow cyborg.

Ajax actually blushed. "Sorry, sir." He glanced at Billie. "Sorry. You didn't hear that, okay?"

"Hear what?" she asked, tongue-in-cheek.

Ajax just stared at her for a moment before he caught on, then he laughed. It was the first real laugh she'd ever heard out of the usually stoic cyborg. She counted it a small victory that she could bring laughter to one of these poor souls who had been taken advantage of so badly.

"Let's find a place to hide and observe," Medeus said, coming up beside her in that silent way of his. "Can you chart what we can see of the system from here?"

"Coming up," Billie said, already having started on that task once the screens cleared. She put up the visual, adding elements as she observed them. "There's a gas giant closest to us, and there's a sort of a pathway that skirts it showing traces of the small disturbances we followed to get here."

"That's probably the trade route, such as it is, for this system. I wonder if everyone here is a pirate or a victim of them?" Medeus mused.

"Most likely, sir. Remember the black system they found over in Alpha sector about ten years ago? Pirate's Paradise?" Jason put in from across the small room.

That had been in the news. Billie remembered the supposedly uninhabited system that had been taken over by organized crime and settled by mob bosses, their cronies and slaves brought in to serve their every need. Slaves brought in by pirates.

It had been a huge scandal at the time. The military had been forced to take action due to public outcry when a group of pirates had attacked a colony just a bit too close to the more populated areas of the galaxy. Arrests had been made. Slaves had been freed and returned to their former homes. Lots of bad guys had been caught, but speculation was rife that many had gotten away. Maybe the refugees aboard the *Tobias Bay* had just stumbled onto where the survivors of that clearance had gone.

"This could be the remnants of that," Jason mused. "Or it could be a copycat group. Either way, it looks like they've set up a smaller version of Pirate's Paradise way out here."

"Smaller, but even from here, I can tell it's not something we can take on alone," Medeus said, his tone thick with anger. "Not with this ship. Not with a cargo of civilians."

All the cyborgs looked somber at that. As if they really wanted to go over to the nearest planet and kick some criminal ass. But they couldn't. It was clear to them all. The *Toby* just wasn't built for that kind of thing.

"Well," Billie said, "if we can't do anything about this, the question then becomes, what can we do with this information? Can we get it to someone, somewhere, who *can* do something?"

The cyborgs all turned to look at her, but she wouldn't back down. She knew what it might mean to them, personally, to go someplace where they could get the word out, but they'd already risked this much. Surely, they could risk a little more to hopefully get Aziner Colony—and any other victims of this group of pirates and thieves—the help they needed.

"That would require us to go deeper into occupied space, where we run the risk of crossing paths with the military," Ajax said, as if she hadn't already figured that out.

"Yes, I know. In fact, I think the military is who we need to contact about this, but we could always do what we did before and have Cordelia pose as captain, right?" Billie asked.

"That wouldn't work if we went through official channels. She doesn't have a captain's license, and in fact, none of the women aboard, except Roxy, actually have space faring credentials. You were only halfway through your coursework," Medeus reminded her unnecessarily. "But you're right. We need to get information about this system, and what we suspect about it, to someone who can do something. We just have to figure out who...and how."

"Can all of you guys communicate silently with one another?" Billie asked. Suddenly, the gazes turned on her were either alarmed, suspicious, or both. She forged ahead with her idea, anyway. "Because, if you could... Maybe we could go someplace where there might be other cyborgs, and you could give *them* the information on this system. And please," she put in, "we're not stupid. Most of us figured you had some kind of secret comm among yourselves. That's okay. We can deal with it."

Medeus cleared his throat, drawing attention away from her with the unnecessary sound. "While your idea has merit, there are a few flaws with it. Even if we can transmit this data to other cyborgs, there's no guarantee they'll be able to somehow insert that data into a place where their commanders might be able to see it and act on it. The probability rises if the hypothetical cyborgs we contact are awake, as we are. In that case, though, we have another issue. I think we would all feel duty bound to help them escape so they could live free. Perhaps offer them sanctuary here on the ship, with us." He paused to meet her gaze. "I doubt that would go over well with the passengers. They're only just starting to get used to some of us." He moved his gaze to the other men in the small room. "And then, there's the issue of how to free these hypothetical comrades." Medeus shook his head. "No, that won't work. We have to come up with something else."

"Right now," Ajax broke in, "we have to get the hell out of here. We've been spotted, and the natives are sending something with a lot of live weapons on it to check us out."

"Shit!" Billie turned back to her board and immediately saw what Ajax meant. It was very far away, but that could change in a hurry depending on what kind of drives and weapons the other ship mounted. "Where to?" she asked, sparing a glance for the captain.

"From here?" Medeus seemed to think aloud. "Sector 27 Alpha Blue," he said rapidly. "It's mostly empty, so use your gut and just take us out of here on the fastest possible route."

"Aye, Captain," she muttered as she ran quick calculations and used those instincts that ran in her family to get a solution faster than any regular navigator. "Check this." She shunted the course data to Ajax even as she spoke. He checked her math and then nodded.

"It's solid, Captain," he told Medeus.

"Lay in the course and jump earliest possible," Medeus ordered.

And…they jumped.

Once in the safety of jump space, where no ship could fire on them or easily follow, Billie breathed a huge sigh of relief. They weren't completely off the hook. If those pursuing them were willing and able to follow, they would still have to deal with them on the other side, but Billie was confident she could get them back into jump space quickly enough to avoid real trouble. They could keep hopping in and out of real space until they lost any pursuit.

But that all depended on whether or not the people who had been sent after them were sophisticated enough to follow. Billie strongly suspected they were not. The cyborgs had computers in their brains, and they'd found it difficult at first to pick up the trail they'd been following. To her knowledge, the technique they'd used was something new. Perhaps it was another of those military things that they had to keep secret, but Billie had never seen what they'd done before and didn't truly understand how they'd come up with the coordinates.

She assumed they knew what they were doing because they'd managed to find something. How they'd found the trail that had gotten them to that pirate system was beyond her skills. She just plotted the courses. She didn't understand every last sensor reading taken at every station on the bridge. Nobody could. Unless maybe they were also a cyborg.

But she had something—something that was still developing—that even cyborgs didn't have. She had that navigator's instinct that ran in her family. Incredibly rare, it was known in space-faring circles that some people just had a knack for finding safe pathways through interstellar space.

Jumping blind, as they just had, she'd relied more on the instinct for where to go than if she'd had an actual destination in mind. Medeus had given her a vector and a general area of where he wanted to come out on the other side, but the actual spot was really up to her, in this instance. She wasn't sure exactly why she'd chosen the region of that massive area known simply as Sector 27 Alpha Blue that she had, but Billie knew that when they came out of jump space, something new was going to present itself. She just knew it.

But Sector 27 Alpha Blue was some distance away, and even in jump space, the trip would take a while. Perhaps that's why Medeus had chosen the far-off destination. Or, perhaps, he'd been there before, and it was the first thing he'd thought of. Whatever the reason, they had a solid fifteen hours before they would begin the transition out of jump space.

"Okay, everybody, stand down," Medeus ordered in a calmer tone of voice. "It's been an eventful shift. I've called second shift up a little early, and I think we should take the time while we're safely in jump space to regroup a bit. When we come out tomorrow, we have some decisions to make. I'll want tactical analysis from helm and comms, please. Nav, you did a first-rate job getting us out of there. Thank you." Billie felt a flush of pleasure at the compliment. "We'll have to apprise the civilians of what we've learned tonight after dinner," he went on, sounding resigned about that particular task. "For now, let's take a short break before dinner to think about what we just saw and what we might be able to do about it, if anything."

The cyborgs nodded agreement and stood from their stations, one by one, as their replacements came onto the bridge. Generally, cyborgs didn't really need much sleep to recharge their biological systems, but they did need some. They could get tired, like anybody else. It just didn't happen very often.

As usual, Medeus was the last to leave the bridge. He waited for Billie to join him then they walked out the hatch together. The second-shift crew would watch over the ship's status while they were in the safety of jump space. As long as there was nothing wrong with the ship itself, all would be quiet until tomorrow.

They walked down the corridor together, and this time, when they reached the end of it, Medeus paused. "Would you like to accompany me to the 'ponics section?" he asked somewhat tentatively. "I want to check on the progress down there, and walking among the greenery helps clear my head."

Billie looked up at him and smiled softly. "I'd like that."

Even Medeus didn't know exactly what he'd had in mind when he'd invited Billie to join him on what was essentially a stroll through the gardens. The new 'ponics section was a special place to him, especially now that they'd made love there. After their encounter, once Billie was asleep, he'd gone back to erase all evidence of their presence before anyone from the civilian crew could notice something amiss, but he would always remember the torrid moments in that darkened cargo hold with joy.

It's where he'd reclaimed an important part of his life from before he'd been made into what he was now. It had been a turning point for him. For them.

Maybe that's why he wanted to go back there. Not just to check on the progress the 'ponics team was making, but to remember those sweet moments when he'd first joined his body to Billie's. Moments that might never come again. *Should* never come again, considering what lay between them. If only he was strong enough to resist the delicious temptation of her.

Being with her was everything he wanted, but all that he couldn't keep. He didn't deserve her goodness, her kind heart, her gentle soul. He was a man of warfare and death. He would ruin her, if he let himself, and he didn't want to do that. Not in a million years. She deserved better than that. Better than *him*.

Of course, she also deserved better than she'd gotten from the people who'd abandoned her on *Eagle Nest Station*. None of the refugees had deserved to be left for the aliens to kill or enslave, or whatever it was jit'suku did with prisoners. So far, in this long war, none had ever come back to tell the tale. It was assumed they were just killed, though there was no evidence either way. Once the jit'suku overran a place, they stayed there a good long time until the humans could mount a counteroffensive and drive them out.

In those places where the jits had been driven away, no evidence of humans remained, so nobody knew what had become of those who had not been able to leave. The jits were fond of issuing ultimatums like the one they had given to *Eagle Nest Station*. It seemed they considered it sporting to allow the non-combatants a good, thorough chance to leave before the shooting started.

Anyone who raised arms against a jit'suku soldier was fair game for shooting back, but they had a rigid sense of honor about those who could not or would not defend themselves—the old, the young and females, in particular. The jits didn't seem to know what to do with female soldiers. They'd been known to pull back rather than harm a woman—if they knew a woman was who they were fighting. Battle armor and space ships made it hard to know whether the human fighters were male or female, most of the time.

Medeus and Billie arrived at the 'ponics section a little earlier than he usually did. The crew was still there, working when they entered, and Medeus's steps faltered just a bit. Billie seemed to notice but stepped bravely into the cargo hold, turning back to invite him to follow. Taking a deep breath, Medeus did just that. He hadn't been thinking clearly—something hard for a cyborg with a computer in his brain—or he would have realized he'd let everyone go early from the bridge after the tumult of the day.

He didn't want to disrupt progress in the new farm area, but he also couldn't leave now that people had seen him. That would be awkward, to say the least.

"Come on," Billie said invitingly. "Have you met Josephina?"

"The woman in charge of the 'ponics project?" Medeus knew the name, and even the face, but had never spoken with the woman. He'd left her to her work the few times he'd seen her in the cargo hold. "No, I have not," he answered honestly.

"I'll introduce you," Billie said brightly. He got the impression she would have taken his hand and dragged him over to the other woman if he hadn't walked there willingly. "Josephina," Billie hailed the other woman as they approached, making her look up from her work. "I'd like you to meet our captain, Medeus."

The shy botanist put down her tools and wiped her hands on the improvised apron she wore. Her smile was genuine as she stepped forward, her hand outstretched and a friendly smile on her face.

CHAPTER 9

"Good to finally meet you, Captain," Josephina said, her voice somewhat timid, though her grip was strong in the brief handshake they shared. "Thank you for letting us set up down here. I've truly missed my plants, though of course, these farm crops aren't exactly what I'm used to working with, but it's great to be back on the job."

"You were a xeno-botanist, were you not?" Medeus asked, just to be polite. He already knew the woman's qualifications. He had access to the records of every living soul on board.

Josephina nodded. "I shudder to think what the jit'suku might be doing to my collection back on the station. It took me years to build up that inventory. All for naught, now, of course." She shrugged as if the loss of her life's work didn't matter, but Medeus knew it had to bother her.

"I'm not promising anything," he told her, "but perhaps you can start anew. There's a lot of that going around these days." He had to smile at the irony, and she seemed to understand what he was talking about. Almost everyone aboard had lost everything and was starting over. Cyborgs, civilians…everyone.

Josephina seemed to take heart from his words, and her smile brightened. "I just may do that. Thanks, Captain." She stepped back, her gaze going to the work happening all around them. "Shall I give you the nickel tour?"

Billie answered for him. "We'd love that. Thanks, Josephina."

They spent the next half hour learning more about hydroponics, in general, and the planting happening here, in particular, than anyone would want to know. Josephina was clearly an expert in her field, and it was also clear that she was teaching many of the young adults about botany and plant husbandry, as they worked. She seemed able to make it fun for the teenagers and younger kids to help out.

There weren't many teens aboard, but enough to make a small gang. It was good to see them working productively and learning something at the same time. If they stayed on the ship much longer, Medeus would talk to Cordelia about the possibility of training them in the space sciences. They might as well learn a profession—something they could take with them after this experience. Billie could teach the basics of navigation, if she was so inclined. Some of the others could teach the kids how to be crewmen aboard a civilian vessel.

There were certifications, of course. The idea would be to teach the older kids enough so that they could pass the tests once they got back to more inhabited space. It would be irresponsible not to hold some kind of classes for the older children to begin preparing for a job when they got older. The littlest kids were already having daily classes. Luckily, a few of the women had been primary school teachers. But the older kids needed more specialized vocational instruction. The cyborgs could help... If the women, and the kids, were willing to let them.

He noticed that Josephina didn't stare at his face the way some of the other women did. She seemed more intent on her plants than the people around her, and she gave every indication that she accepted his differences without comment. He wasn't sure what to think. He'd been so certain that everyone would be repulsed by the way he looked now, but maybe he'd been wrong. Neither Billie nor Josephina seemed to care that he had a giant, visible, hard-to-miss scar over half his face—and worse, two-tone skin, as if they hadn't quite finished Frankenstein-ing him back together.

He felt like something out of an old horror movie, sometimes. Whenever he let himself look in the mirror, really. Which was why he'd banished any mirrors from his personal cabin. He didn't need to look to know that his body—his life—had changed forever.

But these interactions made him wonder if he wasn't being overly sensitive. Maybe it wasn't as bad as he'd feared. Maybe some people could see past the obvious damage. Billie certainly had. And now, this other woman—this scholar of the soil—seemed unimpressed by what he'd assumed was a hideousness no woman could overlook.

When Josephina's impromptu tour brought them to a table where three teenagers were working together, Medeus almost backed off. Billie's presence steadied him, and he decided to brazen it out. These kids were among the oldest juveniles on board. They were quickly approaching adulthood, and they were the target audience for the additional schooling he had in mind. If they were going to interact with the cyborgs aboard, they'd have to get used to the way some of them looked.

Medeus knew he was among the worst looking of the repaired men. Some of the guys could almost pass as fully human if their strength, superior senses, and computing ability didn't give them away. Medeus wasn't so lucky. Quite a few of the men were in similar shape, and the kids would have to realize, sooner or later, that not all cyborgs looked like regular people. Medeus would use this encounter as a test. If it went well, he could move forward with his plans to discuss higher education with the women. If it didn't...well...he'd have to devise some other plan.

"Josh, Magrite, Benny, have you met the captain?" Josephina said as she approached the three youths at the table.

All three looked up, clearly curious as they looked at him. Medeus didn't see fear in their gazes, which gave him the courage to keep going. If they'd looked the least bit scared, he would have backed off.

"Captain Medeus, right?" the girl, Magrite, said, smiling shyly at him. "My mom says you saved us."

"We all saved each other," Medeus replied. "It was really the chief engineer and those who worked on the engines who got us to safety. I just told the pilot where to steer the ship. And Billie here, came up with the courses that we follow. She's our navigator."

"Hi, kids," Billie said, waving to the trio of youngsters.

"My uncle was a navigator," Benny piped up.

"Really?" Billie asked a few questions that the boy eagerly answered.

Benny knew more about his uncle than was in any of the records. Medeus added notations to the personnel files, making special note of the child's family background. As Billie well knew, sometimes, navigation talent ran in families. Benny would be a good candidate to test as navigator material. If he had the knack, maybe Billie could help him learn what he'd need to be a professional navigator someday.

Josh was quieter. As Billie chatted with Benny about his uncle, Medeus could feel Josh's gaze. The boy was staring at Medeus's face. At the scars. But when Medeus chanced a glance at the young man, he didn't look repulsed or frightened. His look spoke of interest. Like he was curious about how the scars had formed.

Medeus called up Josh's personnel file and discovered the boy's father had been a successful surgeon in civilian practice. He'd died two years ago, and Josh's mother had left their colony home to take a job at one of the clinics on *Eagle Nest Station*. She had been a midwife and was currently helping the passengers as a nurse. She'd begun organizing a small clinic of sorts on the *Toby*.

"They didn't finish you," Josh said quietly to Medeus

when he noticed his regard.

"What?" Medeus wasn't sure he'd heard the boy correctly.

Josh moved a little closer. "Your face." He gestured to the scar. "They didn't finish matching your skin tone and regenerating the scar. It only takes an hour or two. I'm surprised they didn't finish."

"How do you know this?" Medeus asked the teenager, surprised by his words, and interest.

"I've been learning from my dad since I was a kid," Josh replied. "Mom lets me help in the clinic here, too. I've always wanted to be a doctor, like my dad. I began studying for the entrance exams when I was thirteen. I know what I'm talking about."

Medeus held up his hands, palms outward. "I don't doubt you, son," he said, falling reflexively into the paternal role he had sometimes taken with younger troopers under his command. "I just wondered how you knew so much."

Mollified, the teenager relaxed. "I could probably fix it for you with the things we have on board. Mom brought some supplies with her. We've got a decent clinic started, and she bought some stuff on Aziner's station to round out the equipment."

"I didn't know that," Medeus replied, astounded by the woman's initiative. He shouldn't be. He knew many of the civilian passengers were quite resourceful.

"You should come by. Our regenerator's slow, but it'll fix you up, and any decent nurse can tune the pigments in synthskin to match your original skin tone. I'm sure we can do something to make it look a little better, at least," Josh assured him.

Medeus was so surprised he asked a blunt question. "And you're not afraid of me. Of the way I look?"

Josh shrugged. "Why should I be? It's just a scar. I've seen worse in my dad's old office when he used to let me watch surgery."

"Gross," Magrite said, handily reminding Medeus that these were still kids he was talking to. Kids. He was talking to.

And they weren't afraid of him. Of what he'd become. The thought almost staggered him. "I didn't mean your scar, Captain, but watching surgery? That's icky," she put in, making a face at Josh.

"Was not," Josh replied instantly, which brought on a short round of bickering among the kids that ended when Josephina whistled loudly to break it up. She was smiling, though, so she wasn't mad at the kids, just doing her job playing referee.

"So, what have they got you doing here?" Medeus asked the teens before they could launch into more arguing, just for the fun of it.

They explained the process of thinning the trays of seedlings they'd gotten from the colony and how they were planting them in slightly larger pots that would be put into the hydroponic system. The seedlings were a starter batch they'd received along with the seeds and selection of other plants. These were lettuce varieties and would grow relatively fast, helping them dial in the new 'ponics settings for optimal yield.

When the crew working in the 'ponics hold started tidying up, Medeus realized it was almost time for dinner. He'd accomplished his original goal of winding down from the tense situation on the bridge, but not in the way he had expected. The teens were lively and engaged, and when Josephina reminded them it was time to head to the dining hall, they kept talking as they walked, inviting Billie and Medeus to dine with them and their parents.

Medeus wasn't sure about accepting the invitation, but Billie seemed to have no compunction about it and accepted for both of them, and her little brother, who would be meeting them there. That's how, a few minutes later, Medeus found himself sitting squarely on the civilian side of the dining hall, at a table with the three teens and their mothers, a couple of younger siblings, Billie and young Sam.

Josh had specifically asked Medeus to sit across from him and his mother, and Billie was at Medeus's side, as if she belonged there, with Sam seated next to her so he could talk with the younger boys who took up that end of the table. Magrite was on Medeus's other side, which surprised him. He'd expected the teenage girl to want to get as far from him as possible, but she'd instead opted to move closer. She'd even introduced him to her little sister, who sat next to her, watching Medeus with a shy smile and kind eyes that just about floored him.

The kids' mothers were at first confused by his appearance at their table, but as soon as the kids explained that they'd invited him to join the families for dinner, they were all that was welcoming. Billie and Sam seemed to set them at ease while Medeus just watched it all, fielding all sorts of questions over the cyborg comm when they saw what he was doing. Luckily, his microprocessors could keep up with several different conversations at once, or he'd have been in trouble with his unexpected tablemates.

"I hope you don't mind," Billie told the mothers for a second time as they settled in with their trays of food at the cafeteria-style tables. "When Josh invited us to join you all for dinner, I thought it would be a good opportunity to make some new friends. I feel like we don't mix with the cyborgs enough, and they're so worried about scaring us half the time, they generally won't make the first move in starting a conversation." Billie smiled to soften her words, and the ladies at the table reciprocated.

"I'm glad you're here," Suzanne, Magrite's mother, said from the end of the table. "All of you," she said pointedly, meeting Medeus's and Billie's eyes, in turn, then glancing at Sam talking excitedly with a boy his own age, oblivious to the undercurrents at the table. "I've been wanting to thank you personally for all you're doing to keep us safe. I'm so glad we were able to cobble together a crew of people who knew how to run this ship. Most of us aren't space certified for anything."

"Well, I have to admit, I wasn't fully certified in navigation, even though I had been learning from my brother and father since I was a kid. I was only about halfway through the formal certification process," Billie admitted.

"Your dad was a navigator?" Benny asked eagerly.

"Yeah, it runs in families, sometimes. Both my older brother and father were what they call natural navs," Billie admitted modestly. Benny looked impressed.

"Don't fool yourself, you've got the talent too, Miss Latimer," Medeus said formally, establishing a professional relationship between them at the same time as paying her a compliment. He turned to the others. "Don't worry about any course Billie plots. She has the magic touch."

"And he has Ajax checking all my math," Billie put in, laughingly pointing with her thumb toward Medeus, seated at her side. The others responded to her humor and laughed along with her.

"Is Ajax also a navigator?" Benny asked, looking around at the cyborg section of the dining hall, probably trying to figure out which man was Ajax.

"He had some nav training in his early career," Medeus answered, "but he's actually a pilot. He's manning the helm station on first shift. Billie's our navigator, and Jason is running comms." Medeus pointed to Jason, who saw the gesture and waved in a friendly manner from across the room as Billie waved at him. Benny and the other teens seemed intrigued, which Medeus took as a good sign.

"Captain, if you don't mind my saying, we could fix your scars at the clinic we've cobbled together," Josh's mother, Evelyn, said quietly. "I'm shocked they let you out of the surgical center with such a lack of care. The alterations might take an hour or two with the equipment we have here. I'd imagine in a military clinic, it would only have cost them a few minutes, which is why I'm so amazed they didn't bother."

Medeus bowed his head, trying to find words to answer her kind offer, but it was Billie who surprised him by answering first.

"They didn't care," she said, anger clear in her simmering tone. "And, in the captain's case, I think they did it on purpose, to mark the fact that such a highly ranked fleet commander was now just a cyborg soldier, like all the others they'd made."

Medeus sucked in a breath. He hadn't realized Billie had figured out so much of what he also suspected.

"To be fair, we all *were* just cyborgs when they first rebuilt us. The CCS suppressed all our memories and everything that made us who we had been. It's only now, years later, that we're remembering what our lives were like before," he said, realizing that everyone at the table was listening carefully. Perhaps they hadn't heard this straight from the cyborg's mouth before. "A lot of cyborgs didn't make it more than a year or two in service, so they probably weren't spending a lot of time on how we looked."

Billie blew a raspberry, which made the kids laugh. "They spent the time on a lot of the other guys. I think the fact that they left you looking so scary was a message."

"To who?" Medeus wondered who she thought the message was aimed at.

"To everyone. The man you were had risen to high rank. You undoubtedly had enemies who envied your position. It could have been done out of jealousy. Or, it could have been done so that people who knew you, or who had served under you, would get the message that you weren't the man you had been any longer." Her insight touched him deeply. She'd put a lot of thought into this, he could tell. "Either way, it was cruel. Why leave you looking half-baked when they made others look almost like new?"

"Does it bother you?" Medeus asked, needing to know.

Billie shrugged. "Not particularly. I mean, I get angry when I think of the way they treated you—and that big scar is a reminder of that—but it's just a scar, after all. It doesn't change who you are underneath."

His heart felt lighter at her words. And the fact that the women and children all around were nodding in agreement meant the world to him.

"In that case…" He made a quick decision. "Maybe I'll

check out the clinic you've put together, ma'am. And, actually… Some of my fellow cyborgs probably need your help even more than I do, if you're willing." Medeus would always put his crew first, no matter what the situation. That's what good commanders did. "I also have to applaud your initiative in putting together a clinic in the first place. Perhaps we can reimburse you for any personal expenditures out of ship's funds. We did rather well in trade at the colony, and we still have some of the precious metals from the comet that we mined."

Evelyn held up her hands, forestalling his words. "It wasn't much. The orbital station didn't have that much they were willing to sell," she explained. "But if we have an opportunity to get more equipment somewhere, I may take you up on that offer. We could use a good diagnostic suite and a few other things."

"Make a list, and we'll see what we can do if the opportunity arises," he told her.

CHAPTER 10

After that astounding dinner, they held a general meeting to discuss the events of the day. It was part of keeping the civilians informed. Sam had balked at being told to go out with the smaller kids when the teens got to stay and listen, but Billie had talked him around and he'd left with the others and a couple of the women to watch over them while they played. Once they were gone, the meeting began.

"Right now, we're aimed for an empty sector where we can regroup a bit before we decide how to proceed," Medeus explained to everyone. "We don't believe anyone could have followed us, but there is a slight chance. Being in an empty sector will help us determine more easily if we were trailed."

"And if we were?" one woman wanted to know.

"Then, we jump to another empty sector and keep doing so until we lose our tail," he replied.

They had a few more questions, but mostly, the discussion ranged over their options on how to get the word out about that pirate system. They couldn't decide anything at that moment, so Medeus let the matter ride. The ladies would discuss it among themselves, and perhaps they would come up with a novel solution. Whatever the case, they had some time to think about things before they made any decisions to act...or not.

After the meeting broke up, Medeus was bemused to find Billie at his side. He'd stayed away last night, but she seemed determined not to let him go a second night without some sort of discussion. He almost sighed. He was weak where she was concerned, but he had to make himself be strong. He didn't want to hurt her any worse than he already had.

He went along with her when she suggested a walk around the ship to the observation area. There was a small domed area at the top of the ship where one could view the length of the ship in all directions...as well as the vastness of space. In jump space, individual stars couldn't be seen, of course, but the view was still interesting as light bent and warped around them.

When they arrived at the observation dome, the place was deserted. The lift made a slight whirring sound as it departed, which was enough to alert Medeus should anyone come up here later. For now, they had the dome to themselves, which was probably just as well. Medeus sensed a confrontation was coming, and it was no less than he deserved. He walked over to one of the benches and sat down. He might as well get comfortable to hear Billie out. He owed her that courtesy, at least.

She faced him, standing. She looked...not nervous, exactly. More apprehensive. She turned away before speaking, and when her words reached his ears, they were devastating.

"I know who you are, Michael."

He couldn't breathe for a moment. She turned to face him, and whatever she saw on his face must have reassured her somehow. She sat down next to him. What was she doing? Why wasn't she running away, or screaming at him? Why did she look so...compassionate?

She took her personal tab out of her pocket and showed him an image on the small screen. It was a flatpic of him—as he had been—standing with Alex Latimer. Billie's brother.

His stomach clenched.

"Alex sent that to me in one of his letters. He was so proud to be first nav on the *Vanguard*. He told me that you and he were friends, of a sort. That you'd shepherded his career and kept him with you as you graduated from patrol ships, and went up the line to your fleet flagship. He respected you, and liked you. You looked out for him and the rest of your crew, he said. You were a good commander." She sounded so earnest it almost broke his heart.

"That was a long time ago. A lifetime ago," he said, looking at the man he had been in that image. It hurt to remember those happier times.

"It *was* a long time ago," she agreed, putting the tab away. "A lot happened between then and now, when you weren't *you*, exactly. But that's over. You remember now. You can be the man you were before. You *are* the man you were before. Just...stronger."

"Being a cyborg is about more than just strength. It's a lack of feeling. A lack of memory." He tried to make her understand. It wasn't that simple. "I honestly don't know what I am now, but I know for certain I can never go back to what I was."

"Okay, then. You can't go back. None of us can. I get that." She looked down at her hands, folded neatly in her lap. Why wasn't she angry with him? He still didn't understand that. Not at all. "What we can do, is move forward. Become something new. Something better. Be our best selves."

He liked the sound of that, but he still believed it couldn't be that easy. "Why aren't you mad at me? I got Alex killed." He couldn't stand it anymore. He had to know.

She turned to meet his gaze, her eyes wide. "Is that what you think?" She shook her head slowly, her gaze softening with tears that didn't fall. "Oh, Michael. No. You didn't kill him. You were his friend. You died with him, if you want to look at it like that. You didn't cause the explosion. You were as much a victim of that ship as he was."

"I was the captain. The fleet commander. I was

responsible for everything that happened. I should have inspected more thoroughly. I should have kept tabs on the situation in environmental control more closely. I should have known what could happen." He firmly believed that.

"Oh, no. No, no, no. You were only human. You couldn't know everything about every inch of that ship, or any other. You trusted the process that designed and built that ship and the people that knew each system to know what worked and what didn't. You were a commander, doing what all commanders do. I don't blame you…" A tear did fall then, tracking silently down her soft cheek. "And neither should you blame yourself."

"But I do." The words were torn from him, and he felt something shift—break—in the region of his heart.

Billie moved closer and put her arms around him, snuggling close. Offering comfort as she tucked herself under his chin, against his chest. She held him for a long time, and he could feel the gentle vibration of her shoulders as she sobbed quietly. For him? For herself? For Alex? He couldn't be sure.

And then… He felt wetness on his own face. From the eye that was still human. And…oddly enough…from the replacement eye that was modeled after a human eye and utilized the tear duct on that side of his face that had not been destroyed. He was weeping. For the first time since he'd been a little boy.

It felt…cleansing. Almost purifying.

Cathartic.

Three point seven nine seconds of tear flow, his processor told him. It was enough to tell him he was still human. He felt deeply—as he had when he was fully human. He might have a processor in his brain now, but he had emotions, once again. He *felt*.

He had doubted it. Doubted himself. Ever since he'd awakened, he'd wondered if he could truly experience emotion again as he had before. He'd felt things. Especially in relation to Billie, but he hadn't been sure if that was just a basal response of his hindbrain, or something more nuanced. More complex.

Now, he knew. He was alive again, as he hadn't been for a very long time.

Billie held him and cried for him. Medeus—Michael—was such a good man. He'd carried such a load of responsibility and guilt on his shoulders all this time. She didn't know how he was even still standing.

"Alex loved being your pet navigator," she said between sniffles as the tears started to subside. "He wrote me so many letters. He sent me flatpics of the places he'd traveled, when it wasn't classified. He told me about his friends aboard each ship, and whenever he spoke of you, he had such respect and admiration in his words. I'm glad you looked after him."

"Not well enough," he muttered, and she could hear the emotion in his husky voice. She thought she was getting through to him, which made all this worthwhile.

"When it comes down to it, you weren't protected by the military the way you should have been. Someone should have realized the danger that design posed long before the ships started rolling off the production line." Billie knew for a fact that several prominent designers had lost their careers over the series of mistakes that had not been caught early enough to prevent the loss of the *Vanguard*. Some even speculated about the errors being the result of enemy infiltration, but that had never been proved.

"It's easy to blame others," Medeus insisted.

"For most people, that's true," she allowed. "But you, Captain, seem to have an inability to blame anyone but yourself. You really need to work on that. You're not responsible for every little thing on this old ship. Just like you weren't responsible for every little thing on the *Vanguard*. No matter what tradition states." Her tone was firm. Her tears had dried up. "It's all well and good to say the captain is responsible for his ship, but there comes a point when you have to be practical."

Surprisingly, Medeus chuckled. "Only you would think nothing of flouting thousands of years of military tradition, for my sake."

She looked up at him, his lips so close to hers as she remained snuggled against him. "I would do anything for you, Michael."

The moment stretched.

Then, his lips found hers, and the kiss took her beyond the moment in time to a place where space and time paused, to take a breather. It was just the two of them, in the darkness of space.

The lighting in the observation dome was kept low so people could see out. Only a faint glow lit the path to the lift and surrounded the furniture, like the bench they sat on. Ambient lighting. Mood lighting.

Between the low lights on the dark floor and the prismatic glow of stars speeding past in warped space above, they were in a no-mans-land of bliss, created, it seemed, just for the two of them. She climbed onto his lap, the flat bench making it easy to move around just the way she wanted as she kissed him deeply.

She was the aggressor, this time. She pushed at his clothing until he accommodated her by releasing his waistband. She pushed his pants downward, rising only for a moment to move her own soft pants out of the way. When she returned, she rubbed up against his hardness, moaning a little as the friction between their bodies did its own work on her senses.

She didn't want to wait. Billie wanted to join with him at the most basic level. She wanted to be part of him as he was part of her…if only for a short while. She wanted the reassurance of his touch, his caress. She wanted that more than anything in this moment.

As the stars blurred and warped around them, she placed herself in the optimal position and pushed downward, sliding him into her willing body. It was heaven. It was bliss. But it wasn't enough.

She started to move, riding him as the heavens whirled around them. She threw her head back and just felt him, grounding her in the maelstrom of space. He was her anchor to reality. Her safe port in the storm of emotion crowding her spirit. She loved him. Oh, how she loved him.

He touched her in ways that made her body shiver. His hands stroked her skin, raising goose bumps wherever he touched, and the soft things he whispered in her ear as he nibbled on her earlobe made her whole body clench with desire.

Raw sounds issued from her throat as she rose to the highest pinnacle of pleasure she'd ever felt. She'd never been in love like this before. Raw. Powerful. *Real.*

Michael was all things to her in that moment. Lover. Friend. Savior. She rode him through the storm of her climax and felt a rush of satisfaction when he joined her in orgasm a moment later. Her eyes closed on the whir of space-time around them, the images too powerful for this moment. The moment when her soul was reborn and her spirit renewed by the most potent feelings she had ever experienced.

She clung to him, her arms wrapped around his shoulders, her cheek rubbing against the side of his head, her lips near his right ear. The human side of his face, by chance, though she loved every inch of him—cyborg or not. She had to tell him, and now seemed like the only time she would have the courage.

She kissed the curve of his ear, whispering her feelings to him. "I love you with all my heart, Medeus. Michael. Whatever you want to call yourself. You're the best man I've ever known."

He stiffened, then relaxed at her revelation, and she thought maybe all would be well. Then, his cock swelled within her, again—too fast for a normal man, but maybe that was another *perk* of being a cyborg—and she realized things weren't just going to be okay. They were going to be orgasmic.

He lifted her in his arms and placed her on the bench,

resting on her back. Her legs were splayed, and he unfastened her top so it lay open, her breasts bare to his gaze—and his touch. He joined their bodies together again, but when she assumed he would take her fast and hard, he seemed to have other plans in mind.

He touched her body with gentle fingers, spending time on the soft skin of her midsection before raising his fingers to the curves of her breasts. Cupping, molding, squeezing gently... And, then, licking, sucking and nibbling in ways that made her squirm. Medeus was a master at learning what she liked and giving her all she wanted.

All the while, his hard cock filled her, moving gently, arousing in slow motions, driving her passion upward, once again. She cried out at one point, and he came down over her, escalating his pace, his utter possession. He gazed into her eyes as he began moving with purpose, and then, when he spoke, she wasn't sure, at first, what was happening.

All she could see was his beloved face silhouetted against the weird star patterns outside the dome. Colors whizzed past. Light bent at odd angles and moved at varying speeds. The one constant was Medeus. Michael. Whatever he called himself. The man she loved.

His features were lit only by the dim glow of the ambient lighting on the floor, which blurred out his scars to her vision. He looked whole. Human. A little cyborg, too, with the enhanced eye and ear on the left side of his face, but in the uncertain light, it all blended together to make him...perfect.

And, then, he took her breath away. As he thrust into her, their desire nearly consuming them, he gave her the gift of himself... Of his love.

"I don't deserve you," he said, his voice low, his breathing rapid. "But my heart is yours, Billie. I love you, too."

She went into climax with a full heart and a sappy grin on her face. The big lug loved her! And he'd picked the most intense moment of her life to say it.

Damn, that felt good.

Medeus had taken the precaution of disabling the lift from the moment he and Billie had started to make love in the observation dome. The moment was too important to take the chance that someone might walk in on them. He could interface directly with the ship's controls from his processor, and he'd done what Chiron had invented—the cyborg equivalent of putting a *Do Not Disturb* sign on your door—to let his brethren know that all was well. He was just busy with his lady and wouldn't take kindly to any interruptions.

He still couldn't believe he'd actually admitted his love for her. Or that she could feel the same about him. It seemed like a miracle. Something he had never expected could happen to him the way he was now. Even more amazing—she knew who he had been and didn't hold it against him. She'd *forgiven* him, for goodness sake.

He'd been responsible for Alex's death—or worse—but she didn't blame him. He still blamed himself, of course, but the pain was lessening. Billie's love and forgiveness were acting on him in strange ways. Helping him. Healing him.

He helped her get dressed again, but neither one of them really wanted to leave the observatory. This space was special. Had become even more special after what had transpired between them. Medeus would always think of this small chamber as the place where his life had started over. An experience he never thought would happen. A gift from the special woman who held his heart.

They sat together, arm in arm, and watched the stars slide by in their unpredictable patterns. Jump space was a special place. *Their* special place, now, and forevermore.

"Do we need to be getting back? Will Sam need you?" he asked quietly.

"No, we have all night. Sam is sleeping over at a friend's cabin tonight. I made arrangements because I knew I'd be on-shift early in preparation for down jump," she replied.

"You know, I really liked Alex," Medeus told her after a few moments of silent contemplation. They were talking in low voices, neither one willing to disturb the intimacy between them with loud words. "He was the most amazing navigator I ever worked with. He had such a knack for finding pathways to distant destinations where others could not. That's why I did everything I could to keep him with me from ship to ship. That, and he had a wicked sense of humor. He would say the most ironic things, sometimes. It was all I could do not to crack up on the bridge." He smiled, remembering some of those times.

"Fleet commanders don't laugh?" she asked, smiling gently at him.

"Not on the bridge," he answered. "Especially not during combat operations."

"I can totally see Alex doing that. He and my dad both had this odd sense of humor that would come out at the most inopportune times," she told him. "Mom used to say they'd be cracking jokes at a funeral, if she didn't keep an eye on them."

"I'm sorry you lost your family," Medeus said, squeezing her shoulders gently. "I'm even more sorry Alex died on my ship. So many lives lost."

"Did you ever see any of your crew again?" Billie asked. "I mean…after. Some of them lived, right?"

"Not crew, no," he replied, suddenly unwilling to mar this experience with bad memories, but Billie persisted.

"Oh. You probably saw others who knew you before." She reached up and cupped his cheek. The one with the hideous scar. "I'm sorry."

"You have nothing to be sorry for," he whispered.

She looked like a thought had just occurred to her. "Were you the only one made into a cyborg from your ship? Was it some kind of sick retaliation from others in the chain of command, who were jealous of your success?"

Medeus sighed. She, of all people, was entitled to hear the full story of how he had become a cyborg.

"On many battle ships, there are special accommodations built into the command chairs. They're like small life pods, designed to close around a seated commander. If there's a sudden decompression on the bridge, they seal and are ejected from their moorings. I wasn't sitting in the chair when the bridge took battle damage. I remember making my way to it, already hurt. I was bleeding and had a few broken bones—my left side had been smashed into a console when we took a brutal hit—but I dragged myself over to that chair, knowing it could save me, if the worst should happen. The battle was ongoing, so I just worked through it, from the chair. It had painkillers at the ready, for just that kind of situation. I used them. I numbed my left side so I could continue commanding the battle."

She turned to hug him close. He wasn't shy about accepting her support. This was a hard story to tell.

CHAPTER 11

"Everything would have been all right," he went on. "I could already see there was an opening in the enemy's defenses. I sent missiles on their way and knew it was only a matter of time before we would win the battle. The missiles just had to get there. But, before they hit their mark, the design flaw in the lower decks caused my ship to explode from within. The command chair sealed around me. I wasn't strapped in. I couldn't manage it with my left arm in pieces. I got thrown around inside the pod, damaging me more, as it jettisoned. I sort of vaguely remember being picked up a long time later. After the battle was over, they followed the beacon on that pod to find me in the debris. I was nearly dead by then, but I remember asking about the missiles, and sure enough, they'd hit the mark and won the day. Otherwise, the jits would have just let me die out there in the debris field. I don't remember much of anything after that."

Billie just held him closer, running her hand soothingly down his back. She lay her head on his shoulder, and somehow, the painful memories were more bearable. They didn't speak for a long time, then she lifted her head and sought his gaze.

"I think you should go public with who you were. Let the women onboard know that one of the most heroic commanders in recent military history is the one guiding this ship. I think it would do a lot for morale." Her words floored him.

"Seriously?" He frowned. "I literally went down with my ship. I'd think that would frighten them more than reassure."

She smiled. "You have it wrong, Michael. I doubt you were aware, but the news covered the plight of the *Vanguard* pretty heavily. Newsies even hounded me for a while, to get my reaction as a family member. They made you into a tragic figure who won a key battle at the cost of his own life. Every member of your crew who was lost was profiled and lauded as heroes. They even ratified a day of remembrance in honor of the captain and crew of the *Vanguard*."

"You're kidding," Medeus said. He hadn't known, but when he consulted his link to the ship's archived newsfeed, he saw the truth of her words. He could scarcely believe it.

"Even before your flagship was destroyed, you were already a well-known figure. Fleet commanders aren't common. Especially ones so young and handsome, *and* capable. You were like a recruiter's dream. They talked about you on the news a lot."

"I never asked for that kind of attention," he groused a bit. He hadn't liked the way the press hounded him on his few days of leave each year. He had never really understood their fascination with him.

"I don't know why I didn't see it before. They didn't change your features. They just left you…unfinished, as Josh said." She looked at his face in the dim light, but thankfully, she couldn't see his flushed cheeks.

In his former life, Medeus had never been one to obsess over how he looked, though since becoming aware of having been made into a cyborg, he had to admit to *not* wanting to be seen. Was that vanity? He wasn't sure. Mostly, he didn't want to see fear in people's eyes when they looked at him.

"All people see is the scar," he said. "The ruined face. They don't see the face as it was."

"Maybe that's why they left you that way. So, nobody would recognize you as the former fleet commander," she reasoned. He nodded.

"It was probably something like that," he agreed.

He would never tell her about the taunts stored in his databanks from the time before he remembered who he was. Taunts by his competitors. His fellow commanders. People who had wanted his job. A few who had wanted to destroy him out of jealousy and took great pleasure in seeing him brought low.

He wondered how those same cowards would feel if they knew he remembered it all. If they realized he was aware and awake, with all the power of his cybernetic implants and newly implanted hand-to-hand fighting skills. He was nearly indestructible now, and if he'd had a mind for revenge, he could do some real damage, given half a chance.

Would his enemies quake in their boots? He thought they might. Lucky for them, he wasn't interested in revenge. He just wanted to live his life—what was left of it—in as peaceful a way as possible. Unfortunately, the Universe, and the jit'suku, seemed to have other plans.

"I like it when you call me Michael, but just so we're clear," he told Billie as they sat together in the quiet. "I'm not really comfortable with the idea of revealing my former identity. Not yet, at any rate. To everyone else, I am still Medeus, the cyborg. Maybe I'll have the courage to reveal my past later, but I'm not sure when. There is, however, one thing I need to ask you about." He cleared his throat before continuing. A totally unnecessary act given his cyborg nature, but it was still useful to buy time. "The thing is, nobody really knows about our…uh…relationship. I mean, my fellow cyborgs know we've been spending time together, but they don't know the full extent. The question is, how would you feel about the civilians becoming aware of our…attachment?"

He was nervous for her response. Would she want to keep

their love a secret? He could live with that, but it would make logistics trickier, if they wanted to be together.

"I don't mind if you don't," she said, smiling at him. "Roxy and Chiron are out as a couple. I don't think it would cause too much of a stir if we were, too."

"What about Sam? Do you think he'll be okay with it?" Medeus asked.

Billie smiled. "In case you didn't notice, Sam thinks cyborgs are *the coolest*." She said that last in an imitation of her little brother's enthusiastic voice. "I don't think he'd mind at all to have you around a lot more. I've worried that he hasn't had many male role models in his life. I think you'd be good for him...if you're willing to put up with all his questions. He's at that inquisitive age."

"I'd be honored, if you're sure you don't mind," Medeus answered, feeling a bit choked up.

"I wouldn't mind at all. I want you in my life. I want you to be comfortable with my family. I love you, silly, and I don't care who knows it."

His heart, which was already bursting with happy feelings, felt even lighter. She didn't mind being associated with him—a scarred-up cyborg. He felt his life had finally started again, after a long delay. His heart was full, his mind was sharper than ever, and he had the woman he loved at his side. He really couldn't ask for anything more.

*

When they dropped out of jump space the next day, there was no sign of pursuit. What there was, much to Medeus's surprise, was a small ship off in the far distance.

"It looks like a troop shuttle," Ajax reported. "But I have no idea where it came from. There doesn't appear to be a warship anywhere in the sector." As their sensors cleared, more of the empty space became visible. "Wait. There's a debris field in the far quadrant. Looks like a battle happened here not too long ago."

"Any life signs in the shuttle?" Medeus asked.

"Just one," Ajax answered quickly. "I think he's..."

"A cyborg?" Medeus asked, sitting up straight in his command chair.

He'd just received the same signal the other cyborgs aboard had registered. A cyborg's call for help along the pathways only other cyborgs could access. Which meant... Was he also awake and aware of who he had been?

A rapid discussion of protocol erupted between the cyborgs of the *Tobias Bay*. They quickly decided to let Medeus be their spokesman with the new cyborg, though they would all listen in on the conversation.

"Cyborg on the shuttlecraft, this is Medeus, Captain of the ship just entering the sector. Are you in need of assistance?" Medeus sent out over the common channel the strange cyborg had been using.

"Cyborg CJ7016," the other responded. "Commanding shuttlecraft Tiberion off the *Botany Bay*, now destroyed. We are in need of assistance. Life support running low. Seven survivors on this shuttle, including myself. The others have powered down to conserve air."

Cyborgs could essentially shut themselves off for short periods of time, allowing conservation of resources, including air. They would only need to breathe once every few minutes to keep their biological systems in functional order.

"Cyborg CJ7016," Medeus replied, "do you remember your name?"

"Name?" The other man sounded confused for a moment, then he spoke in a hesitant tone. "I'm...Alex? Alex Latimer, navigator first class of the flagship *Vanguard*."

"Alex?" Medeus shook his head and his gaze went immediately to Billie. Bright stars! This was going to be difficult, but it might turn out to be good, as well, knowing Billie's warm heart as he now did. "Alex, it's Michael. Michael Bennet."

"Commander Bennet?" Alex still sounded confused. He must have only just awakened recently. "We're in a bind, sir.

Can you help?"

"Yes, Alex. We're coming. Just hang on. We'll dock with you and take you and your brothers aboard."

What followed was a tense hour of maneuvering to get closer to the shuttle. Roxy delivered the news that the *Toby* had just enough room in one of the unused cargo holds to house the troop shuttle, if they could pilot it in with some accuracy. Luckily, cyborgs were good at computation, and Alex was able to get a last bit of energy out of the shuttle's drives to make a clean landing inside the *Toby*.

Medeus went down to the cargo hold to meet the shuttle. He brought Billie with him, unwilling to make her wait to see her brother, though he knew he was taking a chance. Alex might not recognize her, or he might be in really bad shape. Regardless, Billie had a right to see her kin. Medeus respected that.

"I leave it up to you what and when to tell Sam," Medeus said to her as they walked briskly down the corridors.

"If Alex is alive…" she whispered.

"He's a cyborg, now," Medeus wouldn't sugar-coat his words. She deserved his honesty.

"I know, but he's alive." He could hear the hope in her voice and he didn't want to quench that fragile ember. Let her hold to her hope while she could. There was a slim chance this could work out the way she hoped.

Medeus knew Billie was surprised he'd asked her to come along, but she was game. He didn't know how else to prepare her for what they might find, so he said nothing more. When they reached the hold, the doors to the shuttle were just opening, and cyborgs were marching out. Six tall men, who watched Medeus and the other cyborgs with varying shades of wonder, suspicion and confusion. Alex was not among them.

"I'm Medeus," he said, moving forward with Chiron. "This is Chiron. He's been acting as coach and teacher for those of us who are newly awakened. I captain this ship."

One by one, the cyborgs stepped forward, cautiously

giving their serial numbers and duty stations. Then, Alex came down the ramp of the shuttle, and Billie let out a sobbing cry.

"Alex!" she called, and the cyborg looked up across the space separating them. Billie took off and rushed into his arms. Alex caught her, the look on his face going from confusion to understanding in a heartbreaking second, while everyone watched.

Alex lifted her in his arms while she continued to hug him, crying and smiling all at the same time. He carried her down the ramp and into the crowd of cyborgs who all watched with great interest.

"Guys?" he said to the six he had traveled with. "This is my sister, Billie."

Every last one of the six new cyborgs looked at her with dawning understanding. Medeus was sure now, as he hadn't been before, that all of these new men were, indeed, awake and aware.

"Latimer," Medeus called, walking closer to the reunited brother and sister. They both looked up at him. "It's good to see you again, Alex."

Alex lowered Billie to the ground, though he kept his arm around her shoulders. "Good to see you too, Commander."

"I'm just the captain of this old tub now, Alex," Medeus disclaimed. "And your sister is our navigator."

"No way." Alex looked pleased, beaming down at his little sister. "You got your license?"

"Almost. Things happened before I could finish my training, but it's a long story. These cyborgs saved us and took us away from *Eagle Nest Station* before it was overrun by aliens."

"Damn. You were on the station when it was hit?" Alex looked at his sister with concern. "We heard about that, but we were way over in Sector Seven."

"Sam was there too," Billie told Alex. "He's in school right now, but I know he'll be happy to see you. We both thought you were dead."

"I was, for a lot of years," Alex admitted. "I only just started to remember things in the past month or two. I remembered you, Bill, and little Sam, but he was just a baby the last time I saw him."

"He's growing fast," she told Alex with a teary smile. "I'm glad you'll have a chance to know each other now. Thank heavens!" She hugged her cyborg brother again, holding him close while the others made room, giving them a few minutes of privacy...or as close as they could come to it in the cargo hold turned hangar bay.

Medeus addressed the other six cyborgs. "Were you all in Sector Seven?"

"I was in Nine when it started. And before that I was over in Sector Three," one of the men replied. One by one, they each reported where they'd been stationed since the attacks on human stations had begun.

"You men have more up-to-date intelligence than we do," Chiron put in, joining them. "We should probably discuss our situation, and then you can decide whether or not you want to stay with us. We are facing some challenges you should know about before you make a decision."

Billie had finally let go of her brother and they walked closer to the group that was slowly heading for the door.

"If it's all the same to you, sirs," Alex said, "I'm staying, regardless. I won't leave my siblings, now that I've found them. And wherever Commander Bennet is, that's where I want to be."

*

Billie knew the cyborgs were holding discussions among themselves over that private comm they had. An hour passed while the newcomers were both debriefed about what they knew of wider galactic events and brought up to speed about the path that had brought the *Tobias Bay* to this sector.

She was flabbergasted at the idea that Alex had survived the *Vanguard* explosion and no one had seen fit to tell her.

That the military could just hide his existence from his family and turn him into a cyborg was absolutely shameful. She wondered how many more of Michael's former crew had come to the same fate. They would never know for certain, but she wouldn't be surprised if they ran into others at some point in the future. If all the cyborgs were starting to remember, there would be more of them leaving human-controlled space. She was sure of it.

Everything she'd seen of cyborgs told her they were resourceful, competent beings. They had all the ingenuity of their human minds along with the superior abilities of their cybernetic implants. Now that they were remembering who they had been, it would be difficult to stop them leaving, once they saw an opportunity.

Alex and his fellow survivors proved her point. Alex had told them all about the running battle with a superior jit'suku force that had led them to this otherwise empty sector. The jits had been relentless. They had followed each desperate jump their captain had devised, until they had been left with nowhere else to run. Out of fuel and low on supplies, they'd made their stand here, in this empty area.

The only good thing about it—the noble thing—was that they'd led the jit'suku raiding party away from the human settlement they had been targeting. With any luck, the colonists would be able to get reinforcements and dig in their defenses before the jits returned.

Alex and the other cyborgs had abandoned ship only when they had realized the *Botany Bay* was doomed. Other crew had taken the lifeboats and been shot down by the merciless jits. The cyborgs had been somewhat smarter, hatching a much riskier plan. They'd boarded the troop shuttle while still in the hold of the mother ship, then waited for the *Botany Bay* to disintegrate around them. They'd floated away—just another piece of debris. All seven of the cyborgs had powered down so as to avoid detection, and Alex had set himself to power up, only when passive sensors indicated the jit ships had left.

Their plan had been very high risk. The jits could have just destroyed the shuttle for the sake of completeness, once the *Botany Bay* was gone, but they hadn't. The lack of life signs on the shuttle had probably been what saved them. Still, they knew they'd basically marooned themselves in an empty sector of space with no supplies and only a troop shuttle's protection and capacity for life support. Everything about their plan had been risky, in the extreme, but it had worked out.

The jits had killed everyone else. Seven cyborgs were the only survivors of the *Botany Bay*. It was a bit of a miracle, and Billie thanked whatever benevolent powers of the Universe had allowed her brother to not only live, but to be reunited with her and Sam.

Billie had taken Alex with her to meet Sam when school let out for the day. While she hadn't expected to have their family reunion take place in a public corridor, she didn't have the heart to keep the brothers apart a moment longer than necessary. And, maybe it would do the women and children good to see that the cyborgs had been people—brothers, and possibly fathers, husbands, or sons—before being changed.

Alex didn't show his nervousness outwardly, but Billie knew he was a bit on edge when the hatch to the make-shift school room opened and the kids started pouring out. The mothers of some of the youngest were there, in the corridor, ready to meet their little ones, but the older kids just walked out on their own and headed for home.

Of course, when they saw Billie standing there with the strange cyborg, more than a few of them decided to loiter a bit on their way down the wide corridor. Billie didn't really notice them except as background noise. She was more focused on the doorway and watching for Sam to make an appearance.

When he did, his steps faltered at seeing the big cyborg standing next to her. Billie stepped forward a bit and Sam came to her. She crouched down to his level and put a hand on his shoulder.

"Sam, honey, do you remember me telling you about our

big brother, Alex?" she asked gently. The noise level in the hallway dropped, but she noted it only peripherally. Sam was her focus now. Sam and Alex, who moved closer in that silent way the cyborgs had.

"Alex died," Sam said, looking in confusion from Billie to the big man who now stood next to her, and back again.

Billie nodded encouragingly. "They told us he died, but I've just learned, it wasn't true." She stroked Sam's hair, willing him to understand and accept the changes in their big brother. "Sweetie, Alex was in a big space battle and he was hurt really bad. The military doctors made him whole again, but he's a lot stronger and bigger than he was."

"A cyborg?" The wonder in Sam's voice gave her hope, and he couldn't stop looking at Alex with wide eyes.

Billie nodded. "Sam, this is Alex. Our big brother. Except now, he's *really* big. And strong." She released Sam's shoulder as he turned to look up at the cyborg at her side.

"You're really Alex?" Sam asked. She could hear the hope in his young voice, and tears started to gather behind her eyes.

Alex knelt down so his eyes were on the same level as Sam's. "You don't remember me because the last time I saw you, you were just a baby, but I remember you, Sammy. I've waited a long time to see you and talk with you. I hope you'll accept my apology for not coming sooner."

"You were busy being a soldier, and all. I understand about that," Sam said magnanimously. "But I really thought you were dead. That's not nice that they made me think we'd never see each other."

"You're right," Alex replied gravely. "It's not nice at all, but at least we found out now, and I'm here, and I'm not going anywhere without you two ever again." Alex looked over at Billie and she felt the tears fall down her cheeks.

"Come here, squirt," Alex said, using the old, hated nickname of her youth. It had never sounded sweeter. Alex held out his arms, putting one around Billie and one around Sam. They moved into the group hug and stayed like that for a long moment.

All around them in the corridor, Billie knew people were watching the reunion. Word would spread, she knew, and she counted that as a good thing. Maybe their family could act as an example, and bring the cyborgs closer to the human contingent on the ship. Whatever happened, Billie was just grateful to have her big brother back. The three Latimer siblings would have a chance to get to know each other now, which was a blessing.

After the corridor reunion, they went to their cabin and Sam peppered Alex with questions. Alex was a good sport and answered most of them. Billie was pleased to see how Sam took to Alex right away. There was no awkwardness between the brothers, which warmed her heart.

Alex was one of the lucky cyborgs whose modifications weren't all that obvious. Billie readily saw the differences in Alex's height and size, but probably only those who had known him before would realize he was a lot bigger now, as a cyborg. Sam had been just a baby the last time Alex had been home on leave and had no memory of the man he'd been.

In a way, that made it a little easier for the two brothers to meet now. Sam had heard nothing but heroic stories about his older brother, whom they'd thought dead. To have him come back was a joyous thing for him. It meant he wasn't the only male Latimer anymore and Sam seemed to think that was great. Sisters were okay, but brothers were *the coolest*.

Sam had even offered up space in his bedroom—which had been built with two beds to begin with—for Alex to sleep, so he'd be living with his family. Billie loved watching them together. Alex was patient and kind with Sam, even if he was still a bit mechanical at times. He'd only just rediscovered his humanity, so it would probably take some time to get all the way back to human, but with Sam's understanding, patience and love, it was clear Alex had a good head start.

Billie left them to sleep. Sam had an early bed time

anyway, and Alex was understandably drained from the rigors of his day. They both fell fast asleep while Billie puttered around the main room of their suite, tidying up. She even went out for a bit to check on how the other men who had come in with Alex were doing. She discovered that they had been introduced to a few of the other civilians and settled into cabins of their own.

Much later, after Billie had returned to her own bedroom, Medeus came to her. He seemed so serious as he stepped into her room, she walked up to him and laid a kiss on him, like she'd wanted to do all day. When he didn't respond as she'd expected, she drew back to look into his eyes.

"Billie, I know we talked about going public with our relationship. I just want to know—in light of Alex's arrival—if you're still okay with that." She smiled as she met his gaze. "Are you willing for Alex to know about us?"

"Of course," she replied, her heart filled with love for the man who always seemed to put her feelings first. "Alex always respected you. I don't think he'll have any problem with us being a couple. I'm proud you chose me. I'm proud of the man you were, are, and will always be. I love you, Michael, no matter what name you choose to go by." She kissed him again, and he joined in for a split second before pulling back to meet her eyes again.

"That's good, because you know…we cyborgs are always joined via the private comm you've suspected we have. The thing is, when I'm with you, I put up a *Do Not Disturb* notice that all my brethren respect. It's something Chiron came up with when he met Roxy. Only…they all know damned well what I'm up to and with who. So, if you wanted to keep this a secret, we'd have to lay low for a while. Otherwise, I'm afraid Alex is going to figure it out pretty quick. Cyborgs are terrible butt-in-skies."

"So, you're telling me, they know when we're…together?" She blushed a bit at the thought of her intimate moments being cataloged by every last man with a processor in his brain on this ship.

"Yes, I'm sorry." He looked contrite, but then, his eyes sparkled at her. "They know just about everything… Including how very much I love you, Billie."

"Oh…" She thought about that for a moment, then smiled. "That's all right, then."

She kissed him, and they didn't come up for air until the next morning.

All over the ship, cyborgs were well aware that now, two of their number had found love. They were envious and happy for them. And hopeful the other cyborgs would each find a woman of their own to love, and be loved by, in the near future. Now that they had a future—and a past they remembered. Things were really looking up for the cyborgs of the *Tobias Bay*.

#

ABOUT THE AUTHOR

Bianca D'Arc has run a laboratory, climbed the corporate ladder in the shark-infested streets of lower Manhattan, studied and taught martial arts, and earned the right to put a whole bunch of letters after her name, but she's always enjoyed writing more than any of her other pursuits. She grew up and still lives on Long Island, where she keeps busy with an extensive garden, several aquariums full of very demanding fish, and writing her favorite genres of paranormal, fantasy and sci-fi romance.

Bianca loves to hear from readers and can be reached through Twitter (@BiancaDArc), Facebook (BiancaDArcAuthor) or through the various links on her website.

WELCOME TO THE D'ARC SIDE…
WWW.BIANCADARC.COM

OTHER BOOKS BY BIANCA D'ARC

Brotherhood of Blood
One & Only
Rare Vintage
Phantom Desires
Sweeter Than Wine
Forever Valentine
Wolf Hills*
Wolf Quest

Tales of the Were
Lords of the Were
Inferno

The Others
Rocky
Slade

String of Fate
Cat's Cradle
King's Throne
Jacob's Ladder
Her Warriors

Redstone Clan
The Purrfect Stranger
Grif
Red
Magnus
Bobcat
Matt

Big Wolf
A Touch of Class

Grizzly Cove
All About the Bear
Mating Dance
Night Shift
Alpha Bear
Saving Grace
Bearliest Catch
The Bear's Healing Touch
The Luck of the Shifters
Badass Bear
Loaded for Bear
Bounty Hunter Bear
Storm Bear
Bear Meets Girl
Spirit Bear

Were-Fey Love Story
Lone Wolf
Snow Magic
Midnight Kiss

Lick of Fire Trilogy
Phoenix Rising
Phoenix and the Wolf
Phoenix and the Dragon

Jaguar Island (Howls)
The Jaguar Tycoon
The Jaguar Bodyguard

Gemini Project
Tag Team
Doubling Down
Deuces Wild

Guardians of the Dark
Half Past Dead
Once Bitten, Twice Dead
A Darker Shade of Dead
The Beast Within
Dead Alert

Gifts of the Ancients
Warrior's Heart

Dragon Knights
Daughters of the Dragon
Maiden Flight*
Border Lair
The Ice Dragon**
Prince of Spies***

Novellas
The Dragon Healer
Master at Arms
Wings of Change

Sons of Draconia
FireDrake
Dragon Storm
Keeper of the Flame
Hidden Dragons

The Sea Captain's Daughter
Book 1: Sea Dragon
Book 2: Dragon Fire
Book 3: Dragon Mates

The Captain's Dragon

Resonance Mates
Hara's Legacy**
Davin's Quest
Jaci's Experiment
Grady's Awakening
Harry's Sacrifice

StarLords
Hidden Talent
Talent For Trouble
Shy Talent

Jit'Suku Chronicles
Arcana
King of Swords
King of Cups
King of Clubs
King of Stars
End of the Line
Diva

Sons of Amber
Angel in the Badlands
Master of Her Heart

In the Stars
The Cyborg Next Door
Heart of the Machine

StarLords
Hidden Talent
Talent For Trouble
Shy Talent

* RT Book Reviews Awards Nominee
** EPPIE Award Winner
*** CAPA Award Winner

Phoenix Rising

Lance is inexplicably drawn to the sun and doesn't understand why. Tina is a witch who remembers him from their high school days. She'd had a crush on the quiet boy who had an air of magic about him. Reunited by Fate, she wonders if she could be the one to ground him and make him want to stay even after the fire within him claims his soul...if only their love can be strong enough.

Phoenix and the Wolf

Diana is drawn to the sun and dreams of flying, but her elderly grandmother needs her feet firmly on the ground. When Diana's old clunker breaks down in front of a high-end car lot, she seeks help and finds herself ensnared by the sexy werewolf mechanic who runs the repair shop. Stone makes her want to forget all her responsibilities and take a walk on the wild side...with him.

Phoenix and the Dragon

He's a dragon shapeshifter in search of others like himself. She's a newly transformed phoenix shifter with a lot to learn and bad guys on her trail. Together, they will go on a dazzling adventure into the unknown, and fight against evil folk intent on subduing her immense power and using it for their own ends. They will face untold danger and find love that will last a lifetime.

Lone Wolf

Josh is a werewolf who suddenly has extra, unexpected and totally untrained powers. He's not happy about it - or about the evil jackasses who keep attacking him, trying to steal his magic. Forced to seek help, Josh is sent to an unexpected ally for training.

Deena is a priestess with more than her share of magical power and a unique ability that has made her a target. She welcomes Josh, seeing a kindred soul in the lone werewolf. She knows she can help him... if they can survive their enemies long enough.

Snow Magic

Evie has been a lone wolf since the disappearance of her mate, Sir Rayburne, a fey knight from another realm. Left all alone with a young son to raise, Evie has become stronger than she ever was. But now her son is grown and suddenly Ray is back.

Ray never meant to leave Evie all those years ago but he's been caught in a magical trap, slowly being drained of magic all this time. Freed at last, he whisks Evie to the only place he knows in the mortal realm where they were happy and safe—the rustic cabin in the midst of a North Dakota winter where they had been newlyweds. He's used the last of his magic to get there and until he recovers a bit, they're stuck in the middle of nowhere with a blizzard coming and bad guys on their trail.

Can they pick up where they left off and rekindle the magic between them, or has it been extinguished forever?

Midnight Kiss

Margo is a werewolf on a mission...with a disruptively handsome mage named Gabe. She can't figure out where Gabe fits in the pecking order, but it doesn't seem to matter to the attraction driving her wild. Gabe knows he's going to have to prove himself in order to win Margo's heart. He wants her for his mate, but can she give her heart to a mage? And will their dangerous quest get in the way?

The Jaguar Tycoon
Mark may be the larger-than-life billionaire Alpha of the secretive Jaguar Clan, but he's a pussycat when it comes to the one women destined to be his mate. Shelly is an up-and-coming architect trying to drum up business at an elite dinner party at which Mark is the guest of honor. When shots ring out, the hunt for the gunman brings Mark into Shelly's path and their lives will never be the same.

The Jaguar Bodyguard
Sworn to protect his Clan, Nick heads to Hollywood to keep an eye on a rising star who has seen a little too much for her own good. Unexpectedly fame has made a circus of Sal's life, but when decapitated squirrels show up on her doorstep, she knows she needs professional help. Nick embeds himself in her security squad to keep an eye on her as sparks fly and passions rise between them. Can he keep her safe and prevent her from revealing what she knows?

The Jaguar's Secret Baby
Hank has never forgotten the wild woman with whom he spent one memorable night. He's dreamed of her for years now, but has never been back to the small airport in Texas owned and run by her werewolf Pack. Tracy was left with a delicious memory of her night in Hank's arms, and a beautiful baby girl who is the light of her life. She chose not to tell Hank about his daughter, but when he finally returns and he discovers the daughter he's never known, he'll do all he can to set things right.

WWW.BIANCADARC.COM

CPSIA information can be obtained
at www.ICGtesting.com
Printed in the USA
LVHW031700130120
643457LV00015B/1517/P